A WINTER CABIN
CHRISTMAS

ALSO BY MEGAN SQUIRES

Christmas at Yuletide Farm

An Heirloom Christmas

A Lake House Holiday

In the Market for Love

A WINTER CABIN CHRISTMAS

MEGAN SQUIRES

May you never grow too old
to search the skies on Christmas Eve.

CHAPTER 1

*S*amantha Day dropped her handful of loose change into the tip jar, the coins jingling in the glass like the distant chime of a sleigh bell. As she stepped out of line, she caught the gaze of an older businessman waiting near the barista bar, his legs crossed loosely at the ankles, elbow casually perched on the counter. The noticeably high-end suit was an offbeat pairing with the necklace of Christmas lights strung over an expertly knotted tie.

Samantha grinned at the juxtaposition. The lights were the large opaque bulbs, much like the kind that had once adorned her family's holiday tree. Samantha loved those lights and the nostalgia inherent in their vintage appeal.

As though keeping time with the percussive clanking and gurgling from the espresso machine, the light bulbs around the man's neck flickered on and off in perfect rhythm. Samantha adored every bit of the joy-filled scene. Unquestionably, this was her favorite time of year: the anticipated days leading up to December. Storefronts became wintery displays, radio playlists turned into a collection of carols, and coffee cups transitioned from plain cardboard to jolly reds and greens.

The atmosphere always shifted as the holidays approached. Smiles were more readily exchanged, doors more graciously held open. Spirits became abundantly lighter. Samantha's certainly was. Of course, it helped that she had just negotiated a massive recording contract for her dear friend and client, Trish Whitley, something that had been in the works for months. They'd celebrated the night before, popping the cork on the high-priced champagne she'd purchased the day she had agreed to represent Trish. Buying and holding onto a bottle of bubbly for each client was a little tradition Samantha had started at Knight and Day Talent Agency nearly a decade earlier.

"Prepare for success by planning to celebrate it."

The first time she'd heard the saying, Samantha had been a freckled-faced six-year-old, cleats strapped to her feet and shin guards secured clear up to her knees. And the celebration her coach had promised involved a plastic baggie full of the juiciest sliced oranges she'd ever tasted. To some, it seemed small. Maybe even insignificant. But it was the hope of celebration that had motivated her. To this day, Samantha maintained this mantra in all areas of her life.

This morning's celebration came in the form of a peppermint white mocha, extra whipped cream and a generous dash of sprinkles—her favorite holiday drink. Even if she was merely commemorating the fact that she had hit the snooze button two times instead of her customary three, she would take it. Adulthood was full of too many uncontrollable disappointments not to rejoice in the small, daily accomplishments.

"Samantha, your white mocha is up," the barista sang from behind the counter to the familiar tune of *Santa Claus is Coming to Town*.

Pulling up an email that had landed in her inbox earlier that morning, Samantha gazed down at her palm, pretending to ignore the barista's announcement. And just as she'd hoped, he crooned out once more, this time at a volume loud enough for all within the coffee shop to easily hear.

"Samantha, your white moch-*ahhh* is up!"

Rich, booming baritone. *Check.*

Quirky intonation and inflection. *Check.*

Memorable, likeable quality. *Check.*

Sliding her hand into her red leather purse, Samantha withdrew a business card and pressed her way through the pack of customers awaiting their drink orders at the coffee bar.

"That's me!" she hollered as the barista brandished the cup, a lopsided smile spread wide on his face. "Here, let me trade you." She slipped him the thin card and made note of the nametag on his apron. "Corbin, is it?"

The young man nodded—albeit hesitantly—flipping over the piece of cardstock, his brow buckling as he rapidly scanned her information.

"I'm Samantha, but you already know that." She tapped the side of her cup, right next to her name scrawled in black ink. "I'm a local talent agent and I think I have the perfect gig for you, if you're interested. Ever recorded a commercial jingle?"

"Can't say I have," he admitted in a voice much less confident than his earlier melodic tone. "I'm not really sure I've got the chops for anything like that."

Over the years, Samantha had discovered it wasn't at all unusual for people to shrink back when she first approached them. It wasn't so much that they were put off by her boldness. Rather, they often second-guessed their abilities. Insecurity affected nearly everyone like a case of imposter syndrome. It was Samantha's job to push through that initial uncertainty with enthusiasm and encouragement. She was dang good at her job and knew talent when she saw, heard, and felt it. Corbin was a perfect match for the *Country House Kitchen* commercial. She'd bet money on it, even buy the obligatory bottle of champagne as soon as she left the coffeehouse, she was that confident.

"Don't sell yourself short. I'm in the business of noticing talent and I certainly noticed yours." She cupped the steaming coffee in her hands and inclined her head closer. "Listen, no pressure, but if you'd like to hear more about the opportunity, all of my information is on that card."

Corbin slipped it into the wide front pocket of his apron and if he was still riddled with self-doubt, Samantha couldn't detect a trace of it. The full, genuine grin that lifted his features hid it well. "Thank you, Samantha. You know, I think I *will* be in touch. Appreciate it."

Raising her cup in a salute, Samantha backed away from the counter, readying for what inevitably would come next. Like clockwork, a young mother touched her elbow just as she was at the threshold of the café.

"Everyone says she's even cuter than the kid on those baby food labels," the woman spoke in a rush as she flicked through a reel of photographs on her smartphone. "Most beautiful baby on the planet, I tell you. You just have to see her in person. She's a doll!"

And then there was the teenager who had worked a few magic gigs at children's birthday parties, followed by the older gentleman whose dog could bark the alphabet.

There was no shortage of talent within the confines of the coffee shop, and, like she did with every person to approach her unsolicited, Samantha gave them a smile, her card, and instructions to send her an email.

Everybody was gifted in one form or another; that wasn't the question. The root of the matter was that not everyone was a perfect fit for the jobs Samantha had access to. It was like a matching game of cards, flipping over each piece until the perfect pair stared right back up. And when Samantha managed to free herself from the persistent throng of talented hopefuls and her phone buzzed with an incoming email alert, that matchmaking feeling of triumph jolted her more than the shot of the caffeine in her cup.

Seeking the likeness of Mr. and Mrs. Claus for a promotional commercial at Cedar Crest Cabins, a unique lodging experience in the heart of Comfort Valley. Candidates must be available to interview and potentially shoot on location the week of December first through seventh, longer if necessary. Accommodations include room and board, along with all meals and refreshments. Must have prior experience working as Santa, along with available references.

Clicking out of the email, Samantha kept the phone in her grasp as she dialed the number. Unbridled giddiness bounced within her like marshmallows bobbing in hot chocolate.

"Dad!" she blurted as soon as she heard his warm greeting on the other end of the line. She couldn't hide the smile from her voice when she asked, "Any chance you still have that Santa suit?"

CHAPTER 2

"That should do the trick." Noah Jensen gave one final twist of the rusted wrench before scooting out from below the sink like a mechanic rolling beneath a broken-down vehicle. Stretching his shoulders as he elevated from the crouched position, he draped the sodden dishtowel across his forearm and gave Rita Carlos an instructive nod. "Go ahead and give it a whirl."

Like she'd been asked to dismantle a potential explosive, the older woman clenched her teeth, shut her eyes, and gingerly lifted the handle on the faucet. Water poured out in a steady, uneventful stream.

"Hallelujah!" Rita shouted, jerking her hand back and clasping her chest, overjoyed at the sight. "The last time I did that, I looked like I'd been sprayed with a fire hose! Thank you so much, Noah. You're a real lifesaver."

"Happy to be of help."

Noah moved to the kitchen table in the cozy breakfast nook nearby. He unfastened the latch on his hand-me-down toolbox, depositing the wrench next to his father's old tape measure that had a stubborn kink right at the three-foot mark, rendering it largely useless for the majority of Noah's projects. One of these days, he'd go through the contents of the old box, purging the items that no longer held any value. Trouble was, everything that had once belonged to his father possessed some sort of worth—sentimental, at minimum. It was funny how objects could trap memories within them like the pages of a well-worn, family scrapbook.

Had he not caught the waft of sugary warmth first, Rita standing immediately at his back with a plate of cookies would've made him startle. How had he slipped into his thoughts so quickly?

"Take as many as you'd like." Rita nudged her chin toward the tempting plate in her grasp. Soft sugar cookies piled five high made Noah's taste buds buzz. "While the sink might have been out of commission, luckily the oven wasn't," she said with a wink that crinkled the friendly laugh lines bracketing her mouth and eyes. She lowered the tray to the table and brushed her palms together. "Now you sit tight while I grab my checkbook real quick—"

"Oh, no you don't," Noah interrupted around a crumbly mouthful.

"Noah Jensen, you have to let me pay you."

Snapping off another bite between his teeth, he

challenged, "You already have." He lifted the half-eaten treat. "In freshly baked cookies."

"Calories and dollars don't equate." The skin between Rita's brows creased over gray-blue eyes. "That's hardly fair."

Noah knew there was a wide breadth to fairness, like a pendulum that swung out in each direction. The umpire's call during last year's World Series, resulting in a game-ending strike, was fair. Replay after replay deemed it overwhelmingly so.

What wasn't fair was that, after three years of desperately endeavoring to maintain his family's legacy, Cedar Crest Cabins—the Jensen's livelihood and lifeblood—was on the brink of foreclosure. Fairness couldn't be found in any facet of that situation.

"You're sure I can't pay you?"

"I'm sure you *can*," Noah said with a smile. "But I won't accept it."

He took the handle of his toolbox into his grasp and ambled toward the door, as though making an escape could somehow temper Rita's persistence. He knew full well there would be a check with his name on it arriving in the mailbox come early next week. However, if he could stave off her insistence just a while longer, he'd certainly try.

After the sudden passing of both his father and grandfather in a dreadful plane accident in the Sierras, the residents of Comfort Valley showered Noah's family with love and grace, dropping by with piping hot casserole dishes and handwritten cards of condolence. To take anything from the very people who gave his family so much during that tragic time felt close to a crime.

This was Noah's way of repayment; his thank-you in tangible form.

"You'll let me know if that faucet gives you any more trouble?" he asked as he stepped onto the front stoop, careful not to slip on the iridescent sheen of ice coating the mat's fine bristles. Overnight temperatures well below freezing had left behind a frosty layering, as though the very sugar from Rita's cookies had been sprinkled across every outdoor surface.

"I sure will, but I'm confident you fixed the problem. You always do. Thank you again."

"Anytime, Rita." Noah smiled. "And I mean that. I'm just a phone call away."

Scurrying up the path, Noah gripped the toolbox in one hand as he wound his scarf around his neck with the other, tucking the fringed edges into the collar of his goose down jacket. Every year, his sweet grandmother, Kitty, would knit holiday scarves for each member of the Jensen clan, fashioning the most intricate creations with matching yarns and festive patterns. Noah begrudgingly donned the bulky wrap as a young boy. But in adulthood, he had grown to appreciate not only the warmth of the scarf itself, but the loving gesture inherent in each and every purl stitch.

There was no use in denying it—time had turned Noah into a sentimental bundle of mush. Losing the patriarchs of his family exacerbated that. But there were worse things than being in touch with your emotions, he figured.

The loss had noticeably hardened his older brother, Marty. Not that Marty was ever soft by any definition of the word. Growing up, Marty spent more time in the principal's office than in a classroom. He even served a stint in juvenile hall for an impulsive crime that robbed more than just the neighborhood convenience store. It had robbed Marty of a healthy adolescence and their family of normalcy and trust.

Wayward and rebellious, Marty carved a rugged path for himself. One Noah had no interest in following. At one point, Noah had even cautioned his younger brother, David, to do the very opposite of anything he saw Marty do. Apparently, David took that advice on the most literal level by asking out the girl Marty unceremoniously dumped the night of senior prom. Funnily enough, that decision worked out well in the end for David. The wedding band he'd been sporting for the last decade was a testament of that.

Noah snickered to himself as he fit the key into the ignition of his Jeep and the engine roared to life. The Jensen men were as different as flavors of ice cream, and yet here they were, working together to save the cabins. Or attempting to. Just last night, Noah posted an ad on a job website, requesting the likeness of Mr. and Mrs. Claus for a commercial he hoped to film at their mountain lodges. He wasn't sure a commercial was a viable marketing strategy these days, but it had been the first thing the brothers had agreed upon, so he ran with it.

Just as Noah flipped his blinker to exit Rita's street and direct his vehicle toward Cedar Crest, his phone pulsed across the passenger seat. His youngest brother's photo illuminated the screen. *David's ears must be burning,* Noah mused as he pressed his thumb onto the steering wheel button to answer and wait for the call to connect.

"Ho, ho, ho times five, big brother," David greeted jollily through the car's speakers.

Noah chuckled. "Am I supposed to know what that means?"

"It means your ad has been a huge success. We've already got five Santa's committed to coming out the first of December. And based on the initial response, I figure we'll easily fill all ten cabins by the end of the week. Your perfect Mr. Claus is bound to be in that group."

"Wow. Not gonna lie—that honestly sounds a little overwhelming. Can you imagine all of the milk and cookies we're going to go through?" Noah teased.

"Not to mention coming up with parking for the sleighs, along with a place for the reindeer," his brother rallied right back. "And the elves! I totally forgot about the elves."

"What have we gotten ourselves into?"

"Hopefully a very real opportunity to save the cabins," David spoke with a resigned sigh Noah could sense, even through the phone. "At the very least, I figure we can cash in a Christmas wish with each and every Santa that sets foot on the property. Couldn't hurt, right?"

Noah completely agreed. Especially during this magical time of year, a little wishful thinking never hurt.

CHAPTER 3

*E*ven though there was a sturdy office wall separating them, Samantha could still hear the vibrating murmur of Oliver's voice, like the low hum of an idling car. She needed to catch him between phone calls, but Oliver Knight was a verbose man with a talent for turning five-minute conversations into hour-long monologues.

Sometimes, Samantha wondered if that had been the real reason for their divorce three years earlier. There were days when she felt she couldn't get a word in, and that feeling of not being heard eventually shifted into not being seen, either. She'd been invisible as a wife and soon realized Oliver was more married to his job than he ever was to their actual union.

They didn't work well as spouses, but as colleagues, they thrived. Their talent agency was notably the best in the Sacramento Valley, with an impressive client list and a calendar packed with promising auditions. It was that solidly filled schedule that made Samantha's stomach knot. And when the lull she'd been so patiently waiting for finally came, she bounded from her desk chair and rushed over to Oliver's office, eager to seize the fleeting opportunity.

"Knock, knock," she said through the partially opened door. Oliver reclined at his large mahogany desk, snakeskin leather shoes propped up on the glossy, wooden surface, arms bent behind his head as though lounging on a chaise in the sun. "Taking a little breather?" she asked in jest as she edged into the room.

"Got another call in five," Oliver replied, dragging his legs from the desk to sit upright. "What's up, Sam?"

In the workplace they were equals, so Samantha couldn't make sense of her rising nerves. She swallowed around the lump forming in her throat and said, "I'll be taking some vacation time and just wanted to give you a head's up. Kara is handling all of my client portfolios and I've briefed her on upcoming auditions, so you won't be impacted by my absence at all."

The last thing Samantha wanted was for her sudden plans to burden anyone at the agency. She had made certain all of her ducks were in the neatest of rows.

"I can't even recall the last time you took a vacation." Oliver's head shook slightly, causing a lock of his hair to fall over deep set, light blue eyes. It was that alluring, almost captivating gaze that first drew Samantha in when they'd started dating as young interns, fresh out of college. They'd met once as teenagers when their lives had crossed paths in what some might call an act of fate, but it wasn't until they were older and worked side by side that she'd fallen for him. Oliver was intense and focused, and that had been attractive to no end.

"It's not exactly a *vacation*-vacation," Samantha explained. "More like a working holiday."

"Anywhere fun?"

She knew his interest was manufactured, but it was polite all the same. "Cedar Crest Cabins up in the Sierras. Near Comfort Valley. You heard of them?"

"Believe it or not, I actually have. My parents used to take me every year. They had the best Santa Claus and would do this whole Christmas concert. I always wondered what happened to those sleepy little cabins. I heard they've been struggling since the construction of the bypass. Can't imagine they get much traffic up their way anymore."

Samantha propped her hip against the doorframe and folded her arms over her chest. "I think you're right about that. In fact, that's the whole reason I'm going. Mom and Dad will be auditioning as Mr. and Mrs. Claus for a commercial filmed at the cabins. I figured I would tag along and coach them a little. Help them land the gig however I can."

A small smile drew up the corners of Oliver's

mouth. "Your dad hasn't played Santa since…" His voice fell away, empathy shrouding his eyes.

"Since the children's hospital," Samantha finished for him. "I think it's finally time to dust off the old, red suit and give it another go."

"I'm glad to hear that, Sam. I really am." Clamping two palms onto the desk, Oliver glanced toward his phone like it might ring at any given moment. "Listen, don't worry about the agency while you're away. Have Kara come to me if she needs anything. Just focus on enjoying the time with your parents. And have fun at those cabins. As I remember from childhood, Cedar Crest really is an enchanted place."

FOLLOWING BEHIND THE SNOW PLOW MADE FOR A terribly slow drive, but gratitude swelled in Samantha's chest all the same. Chains hadn't been on the short list of items she'd tossed into her sedan earlier that morning when she packed for the somewhat spontaneous getaway. In fact, it had been so long since she'd even ventured up the hill to the Sierras, she'd completely forgotten chains were often a requirement on this twisty stretch of mountain road. She took the freshly cleared lanes as a sign that she was indeed on the right path, both figuratively and literally.

Glancing toward the cockeyed rearview mirror held on by a crude strip of duct tape, Samantha verified that her parents followed closely behind. Her dad's diesel truck sat higher than her small coupe, and the fresh wreath fastened to his grill met her gaze each time her eyes flitted toward the mirror.

Her parents, Joan and Jack, loved the holidays. They were the type to decorate their tree the day after Halloween and leave it up until Valentine's Day came around the following year. Christmas was always more than just a week's worth of celebration in the Day household. It was a full season, month upon month filled to the brim with holiday merriment.

Of course, it helped that her father bore an uncanny resemblance to jolly, old Saint Nick. Even as a boy, the apples of his cheeks were the perfect ruddy shade, like he'd been playing with his mother's pot of pink rouge. And when Jack smiled, they rounded just so and pushed up into crystal blue eyes, hooded with bushy brows that, over the years, had turned a frosty silver. He was blessed with a full, thick mane of hair that he would cut every January and then let grow the remainder of the year. Come Christmastime, it fell just below his shoulders in the most handsome, snow-white waves, a perfect match to the beard that hung several inches beneath his chin. While many men nearing seventy might grow frustrated at a little excess weight around their middles, Jack welcomed his "spare tire." Every bit of his appearance was authentic, a genuine replica of the magical man he often portrayed during the holiday season.

Joan made for a believable Mrs. Claus, but it was

Samantha's father who consistently stole the show. She just hoped he'd be able to pull it all off one more time.

Keeping her eyes trained forward, Samantha studied the surrounding landscape. When she had looked up the cabins online the night before, one consistent complaint was that the place was a little tricky to find. The exit snuck up after a blind corner and more often than not, guests missed the turn on their first pass. Apparently, even GPS wasn't any better at successfully guiding drivers toward the destination. Samantha didn't want to miss it, so she squinted her eyes, turned down the volume on the radio dial, and lifted her foot from the gas pedal to ease off her speed.

She'd been so intensely focused that the two loud honks from her dad's horn made her leap right out of her skin. Her gaze darted to the rearview mirror where she could see her mother making huge flapping gestures with her arms, indicating an immediate right turn that Samantha would've surely missed otherwise. Cranking the steering wheel, she nearly took the surprise corner on two wheels. Tires skidding, the car moved sideways on the sleek roadway for several weightless seconds before the front end of her vehicle finally pointed forward, the back continuing to fishtail and flail about. Everything in her knew not to over-correct, but nothing could be done to stop that knee-jerk reaction. With one erratic twist of the steering wheel, the compact vehicle spun out, sailing off the frozen asphalt and careening into a powdery embankment.

Before Samantha had a chance to replay the string of disastrous events in her head, her father was at the driver's side door, tapping on the glass with his knuckle, eyes wild with concern.

"Sammy! You okay?" His shout was muffled through the glass separating them. "You're not hurt, are you?"

The vehicle had come to rest at an angle, leaving half of the car buried in chalky white, while the other side—the one Samantha was on—remained mostly perched above the wall of snow.

"I'm fine," Samantha hollered back.

She gripped the door handle and pushed, but the weight of packed snow secured it stubbornly in place. On the outside, her father pressed a palm to the frame and another on the handle and tugged mightily as Samantha pushed, and together, they freed the door from its stuck position.

Snow spilled into the vehicle, covering the floorboards with frozen slush.

Jack grasped his daughter's hand and hauled her to her feet. "I just took the chains out of my truck last week to use on the tractor, otherwise I'd pull you out of here myself. I can see if someone at the lodge might be able to help us out. I'm sure we're not the first ones this has happened to."

"You're *not* going to do that, Dad." Samantha

reached into the backseat and gathered her duffle bag and backpack, then slammed the door into place.

"I'm not?"

"No. I will handle this. All you need to focus on is getting into your Santa zone," she instructed as the two walked back to her father's idling truck. Gritty snow mixed with asphalt crunched beneath her boots in a sludgy, gray mire. She had been so toasty warm within the confines of her car, but now the alpine air cut through her as it stung her cheeks and nose. Securing the belt of her jacket tightly around her middle and holding her duffle bag close, she picked up a jog and joined her mother in the truck.

"You okay, sweetheart?" Joan slid to the center of the bench seat to make room. "Your car okay?"

"I'm fine. Car's fine," Samantha answered in a breathy huff, more frustrated than embarrassed by her less than stellar driving abilities. She deposited her things by her feet and pulled the seatbelt across her body. "I'll call a tow truck this afternoon and get this all taken care of. But right now, we need to get you guys checked in. Don't want to be the last to the party."

"Oh, is that what this is?" The corner of Joan's mouth bent upward. "A party?"

"Of course." Dipping her hand into her backpack, Samantha withdrew a bottle of her mom's favorite champagne. "And I even brought the bubbly," she said, swinging the bottle side to side.

"You're *that* confident we're going to land this audition, huh?"

"Absolutely, I am."

Joan forced a small smile. "As our daughter, aren't you obligated to say that?"

"I was obligated to say your chicken parmesan was better than Oliver's mom's, even though she grew up in Italy and runs her own restaurant. But I'm not obligated to say you're the best Mr. and Mrs. Claus I've come across in my decade as a talent agent. That is just a tried and true fact."

"Not tried very recently, though." Jack's voice was resigned and soft.

"I'm not worried about that one little bit. It'll come back to you," Samantha assured. "Like riding a bike."

"Or a sleigh," Joan played along.

"Just as long as Sammy's not the one driving it." Jack shot his daughter a teasing look across the cab, his eyes twinkling with mischief.

"I deserved that," Samantha said through a laugh. "But you both deserve this opportunity. More than anyone I know."

CHAPTER 4

"I put the Kringles in cabin four and Sinterklaas in cabin three." Vera Jensen moved the mouse across the computer screen to click out of the booking calendar. "That leaves cabins five, six, and seven for Father and Mother Christmas, St. Nick, and the Clauses." With a sputtering sigh, Vera collapsed onto the metal barstool behind the counter, her fringed, wheat-blonde bangs lifting from her forehead from the breath. She placed her hand on the curve of her protruding belly and exclaimed, "And as soon as I get them checked in, I'm officially going into hibernation!"

Noah couldn't blame Vera for her exhaustion. He was dog-tired too, and he didn't have the justification of being eight months pregnant like his sister-in-law. It had been a whirlwind weekend for all as they readied the property to operate at nearly full capacity, something that hadn't occurred in, well, Noah couldn't even recall the last time. If he thought on it long enough, he could pull up vague childhood memories of families milling about, each member dressed in cozy holiday attire, Christmas carols ringing through the mountain air with the rich scent of mulled cider and hot chocolate flavoring the scene.

Sometimes he wondered if the particular vision was derived from a movie or holiday play he had once watched, that type of magical setting only existing in something fabricated. But Noah was aware that at one point in time, the Cedar Crest Cabins were a sought after destination, maybe even a holiday tradition for some. He had a collection of fuzzy memories of the lodge's parking lot crowded with cars, fresh Christmas trees strapped to rooftops. With a cut-your-own tree farm just ten miles up the road, their cabins made for a perfect holiday getaway.

But over time, the trees were logged and the highway rerouted, setting into motion a snowball effect that left their cabins empty and their bank account in a similar condition. Was he really naïve enough to think a Christmas commercial could truly restore their lodge to its former holiday glory? The more he let the idea tinker around in his mind, the more he felt massively out of his depth.

"Hey, Noah? Any chance you can manage the desk for a few minutes while I visit the ladies' room?" Vera slinked down from the chair and waddled closer to her brother-in-law who stood at the end of the long, wraparound counter that served as the check-in area. "This baby will not get off of my bladder and I'm about to pop."

Noah didn't need to be asked twice. "Sure thing. Cabins two, three, and four are still vacant?" he clarified.

"Five, six, and seven," Vera corrected, her feet shuffling in the direction of the restroom. "Plus cabin eight, but I haven't finished with decorating that one, so let's hold off on assigning it for now. I'll be back in five. Promise."

"Take your time," Noah assured. "I've got this covered."

Vera gave Noah a squint that indicated she didn't put a whole lot of faith in his words, but left him to the front counter all the same.

"Five, six, and seven," Noah recited to himself in a whisper.

He was good at maintenance when it came to broken water heaters and squeaky hinges, less confident in maintaining bookings and schedules. But everyone had to pull their weight if the cabins were to succeed. It was the very reason his grandmother hadn't left the main kitchen in twelve hours, his mother, Audrey, sequestered herself in the laundry room with quilts, linens, and towels, and David ran the plow machine day and night. Even Marty toed the line, making the necessary calls and sending follow-up emails to the production team in charge of filming the commercial. It was all hands on deck, every Jensen needed.

Taking up position behind the counter, Noah peered out the frosted paned windows, noting a large, red truck chugging up the drive. It was silly to be nervous—Noah knew that—but this was not his wheelhouse and anxiety coiled his stomach like a peppermint twist.

"Welcome to Cedar Crest Cabins," he rehearsed softly, the words stilted and wooden. "Welcome to our cozy mountain getaway. We're so glad you're here," he tried again. It was of no use. He sounded like a robot.

Noah was just about to practice his greeting one more time when the entrance door creaked and then flew open, letting in a blast of frigid air that swirled into the lobby with gale-wind force. The crackling fire he'd built in the stone hearth earlier that morning flickered and quickly faded as the rush of cool air quenched the flames. Despite the extinguished blaze, Noah's face heated up the moment his eyes locked in on the woman entering the room.

She was mid-conversation, her head inclined toward an older couple at her back, her voice melodic and sweet, like orange blossom honey. Blonde hair cascaded well past her shoulders in loose, flaxen waves that brushed along a wool pea coat, and when Noah's gaze connected with her jade-hued eyes, that whoosh of air from earlier reenacted in his lungs.

"We're here!" she announced in a sing-song, slightly off-key voice. All of Noah's earlier preparation served no purpose as she bounded up to the counter and settled a canvas duffle bag onto it, bypassing a formal greeting. "Sorry we're so late, but we're finally here now and that's all that matters, right?" Her lips spread into a broad smile. "Checking in for Days."

"How many?" Noah moved the mouse across the pad to stir the computer to life. He thought it odd that his throat felt tight and his heart beat loudly in his ears.

"There are three of us."

"Oh, I'm sorry. I meant how many days?" he corrected himself, connecting glances with the woman again. She was breathtaking, almost intimidatingly so, with her calm confidence and sunny disposition.

Her eyes rounded, and she began to speak slowly. "Three Days: Samantha, Jack, and Joan."

Noah's lips pressed together. "Hmm. The only reservations I have on the calendar are for one-week stays."

"That's correct." She nodded swiftly. She popped up onto her tiptoes to glimpse the screen. "We'll be here for one week."

"I think I'm misunderstanding. I thought you said you were checking in for three days."

"Yes. Three Days: myself, my mother, and my father." She swiveled to point to each individual as she spoke. "And we'll be staying at the cabins for one week. Three Days. One week."

"I think it would be helpful to note that our last name is Day," the older woman finally clarified, edging her way up to the counter, her face alight with a playful grin. She was shorter, with hair Noah figured was once the same shade as her daughter's but had faded to more of a silver tone in her twilight years. "And I can't tell you how many times it has led to silly little misunderstandings like this one."

The gentleman chuckled at their back, three short bursts Noah swore sounded just like *ho, ho, ho.*

"One thing we should also bring to your attention is that Samantha crashed—"

"The party!" the young woman cut off, slamming her palms onto the counter with a jarring clap. "I totally crashed their party. I realize the audition only calls for a Mr. and Mrs. Claus, not their tagalong elf." She waggled her head and smirked. "You might not have me on the reservation, but we'll all be staying in one cabin. I hope it's not too much of an inconvenience."

"The particular cabins we have reserved for this are really only comfortable for two."

The letdown in that information dropped Samantha's shoulders several inches but she appeared to recover from the disappointment quickly. "That's completely fine. I can sleep on the couch. Or a cot. Whatever you have available."

"We actually have an entire cabin available!" Noah supplied cheerily. "Cabin number eight." He peered around the woman. "And Joan and Jack, I'll put you both in cabin seven, right next to your daughter."

Samantha's hand moved to the backpack shoved

high on her shoulder. "That sounds great. What'll that be? Do you take credit cards?"

"We do, but this is on us. All part of the auditioning process."

"I can't ask you to—"

Ignoring her protest, Noah grabbed two keys from the brass hooks on the wall behind him and stepped out from the counter. "I can show you to your cabins now, if you'd like. And I'll help with your bags."

"That would be lovely." Joan paused, searching out a name.

"Noah. Noah Jensen." He extended a hand to shake both Joan and Jack's, then stopped suddenly before reaching toward Samantha's. His palm had dampened with sweat. Thankfully, she just lifted her hand in a small, fluttering wave and grinned.

"Nice to meet you, Noah," Joan spoke for her family. "I can't tell you how happy we are to be here."

Noah didn't voice that he was equally happy about their arrival, knowing that information was absurd to admit aloud. Sure, he'd met beautiful women before, but there was an intriguing quality to Samantha that pulled him in. Resurrecting Cedar Crest was Noah's priority, certainly not resurrecting a love life that had become altogether nonexistent in recent years. He wouldn't let his mind go there— couldn't let it—and yet he worried he wouldn't be able to keep from slipping into territory he had no business exploring.

CHAPTER 5

*S*amantha found herself staring at the bare evergreen, her eyes impulsively tugged in the direction of the equally broad and towering man beside it.

Noah Jensen was a looker. That was a certifiable fact. He had a classically handsome face and, had his headshot landed on her desk, Samantha would have agreed to represent him on the spot. There was that marketable, strong jaw with the perfectly placed depression in the middle of his chin. Full lips—the bottom a touch poutier than the top. Eyes of corn-flower blue, both intense in connection and yet somehow approachable all the same.

It was his sheer size that made her breath falter when she first set foot in the lobby and glimpsed him standing on the other side of the reclaimed wood counter. He was easily a full foot taller than her petite five-foot-four frame, and yet, even with that imposing stature, Noah came across as nothing but warm and familiar. A gentle giant of sorts with a striking appearance that would make even a nun weak in the knees.

Samantha made sure to lock her own knees into place as she stood across from Noah within the confines of the quaint rental cabin. When he'd dropped the keys into her open palm and their fingertips brushed, her heart had fluttered like the rapid wings of a caged bird. She knew it was silly to react in this way. In her line of business, attractive people surrounded her daily. But that didn't necessarily mean she was attracted to them, not in the way she found herself gaping at Noah as he rattled off details regarding the commercial auditions. Details she needed to pay attention to, but for the life of her couldn't, not with that dimpled grin pulling at his mouth and muddling her senses.

"I'm sorry about the tree," he said, drawing her out of her thoughts.

"The tree?"

Noah waved a hand up and down the branches, dense with vibrant, green needles. "That it hasn't been decorated yet. I'll see if I can locate the box of ornaments and lights and drop it by this evening. I'm sure it's just in storage."

"It's no problem," Samantha said. "Honestly. I didn't expect a cabin, much less my very own Christmas tree. I realize what an imposition this is, me just showing up here completely unannounced. You really don't need to put yourself out more than you already have."

"It's not an imposition at all!" Noah interjected eagerly, his words overlapping hers. As though moderating his enthusiasm, he added, "We have the space."

"I'm glad you do." A smile held on Samantha's lips. "Thank you again, Noah. Your hospitality doesn't go unnoticed."

"You are most welcome." He paused where he stood, eyes tightened in exploration of her own. Samantha shifted under his stare, her pulse thrumming wildly like the chorus of *Little Drummer Boy*. There was a moment of quiet between them before Noah appeared to locate his words. "So, dinner's at 6:30 in the lodge dining room." He scratched the back of his neck. "It used to be an actual restaurant, but our chef quit back in the nineties after some silly dispute with my grandfather about cutlery. After that, we decided to just rent it out for local events. Wedding receptions. Church meetings. Things like that. But Grandma Kitty made a generous amount of French venison stew that she can't wait to share, so we'll use this opportunity to gather and go over tomorrow's auditioning process."

"I'll be there." Samantha nearly licked her lips. "You had me at venison stew. My favorite."

"Really?" Mouth hooking into a lopsided grin, Noah's shoulders shrugged up to his ears as he fit his hands in his pockets, looking surprisingly boyish. "I told Grandma Kitty it was probably the worst possible meal one could prepare for a room full of Santas. I mean, what with the reindeer thing and all."

"Oh, goodness." A bursting laugh parted Samantha's lips in a sputter. "I didn't even think of that!"

"Right? I mean, I get that this is just an acting job, but some seem to take it pretty seriously. Did you see the full-sized sleigh in the parking lot? It looks like the real deal."

"My guess is this is more than just a job for the good majority of them. For my mom and dad it is, at least." Samantha's voice trailed off softly and she found herself fidgeting with her hands, suddenly feeling like she'd shared more than necessary. Even still, she continued, "There's something about portraying Santa Claus that is different from any other acting gig. There's magic and tradition. A rich history to preserve."

"Just like these cabins." Noah shared the sentiment in a wistful tone that matched Samantha's. "It's honestly the reason I thought the man in red would be the best spokesman for them."

"I couldn't agree with that decision more."

"Anyway." He smiled and shuffled a few steps backward toward the door. "I'll get out of your hair, but if you need anything, please don't hesitate to ring the front desk. Someone from the Jensen clan will be at the ready and willing to help."

Samantha was perilously close to asking for the name and number of a local towing company, but that wasn't the note she wanted their introduction to end on, one where she admitted she had careened her car right off the road and into a wall of snow. Instead, she thanked Noah once more, following closely as the door slipped shut behind him.

Rotating, she pressed her spine against the solid wood and sighed with delight. In a word, the cabin was rustic with its knotty paneling and hand-hewn log furniture. A generous quilt of blue and green tartan plaid adorned a queen-sized mattress and throw pillows in similar shades made the freestanding loveseat the perfect place to cozy up with a beloved book. There was a stuffed bear with wiry black fur perched in a leather armchair off to the side and a wooden bowl teeming with large, scaly pinecones rested in the very center of a coffee table. A coffee pot, microwave, and small fridge made up the entirety of the kitchenette area, admittedly more amenities than Samantha expected for a cabin of this limited size.

Even without the Christmas tree, the space boasted of holiday warmth. Some of that had to do with the mountain view just outside the window. Undulating, snowcapped peaks created a saw-toothed horizon that felt anything but harsh. The ridge of blue spruces following the same jagged line softened the scene, their branches weighty with layers of brilliant, alabaster snow. As though pulled from a fairytale, a chickadee flitted about on the other side of the glass, coming to rest on the sill, head cocked as its beady eyes locked in on Samantha's. It warbled a delicate trill in greeting before pulsing its tiny wings to take flight.

Samantha clutched her hands together, bursting with delight. She was so grateful for the job opportunity for her parents, but an equal sense of appreciation swelled within her. Oliver was right—it had been much too long since she'd taken a personal day, let alone any vacation time. Right then, Samantha made a small promise that she would bask in all this time away had to offer, secretly hoping it involved more encounters with Noah Jensen.

CHAPTER 6

*N*oah had roughly two hours until dinner, scarcely enough time to head into Comfort Valley to pick up a new dryer vent connector from Hal's Hardware. Snow had fallen steadily all afternoon, so he accounted for the reduced speed on the roadways, knowing he couldn't zip in and out of town like he often did under clearer skies.

Per Vera's text in their family chat, all Santa hopefuls were finally checked in and settled, news that also worked to settle Noah's own nerves. His stomach had been twisted and wrenched tight all morning—that was, until it completely unwound and fluttered when he'd met Samantha.

It wasn't just butterflies inhabiting his stomach now; it was an entire flock of hummingbirds, their vibrating, quivering wings making his gut feel weightless and woozy. When was the last time a woman had had that effect on him?

He prided himself on keeping his cool. That's who Noah was—the steady, dependable Jensen. Marty was impulsive. David was the jokester. But Noah, he was rational. Logical. But there was nothing logical about the way his pulse quickened at the mere thought of Samantha's soft, wavy hair or the way one eye squinted a touch more than the other when pushed up in a smile.

He'd replayed their entire exchange in his head the whole time he worked on the malfunctioning dryer. Did he maintain eye contact too long? Not long enough? Was it really necessary to tell Samantha about the history of the restaurant? Was she even interested in what he had to say? Emptying the lint trap, he had huffed an incredulous sigh, scattering bits of fluff about the laundry room in a swirl of fuzzy cotton.

"Pull yourself together, Jensen," he'd admonished, ultimately deciding a drive into town might serve as a necessary escape from the stubborn thoughts plaguing him. He had just locked the driver's side door of his Jeep into place when the phone in his back pocket vibrated with an incoming call. He didn't recognize the number on the screen, nor the area code, so he answered the formal way he often did, figuring it was likely someone in search of a handyman.

"Comfort Valley Repair Resource," he greeted, wedging his cell phone between his jaw and shoulder as he angled the vehicle out of its resting spot.

"Um, yes, hi," a woman's pleasant voice met his

ear. "I'm not even sure I have the right number for this sort of thing, but I've called two towing companies already and struck out both times."

"You're looking for a tow?" Snow fell at a more vigorous rate now, so Noah flipped on his windshield wipers to scrape the flakes out of his line of sight. "I can probably help with that."

Her relief was palpable, even through the phone connection. "You can? That's wonderful!"

"Where are you located?" Noah gently pressed his foot to the gas, easing down the stretch of drive that connected their mountaintop cabins to the highway. He loved this expanse of road with its towering conifers hemming in the lane, but he also knew how easy it was to spin out if you didn't take your time and the necessary precautions to maintain control in inclement weather.

"Are you familiar with the Cedar Crest Cabins?" the woman asked.

Noah stifled a chuckle. "I am."

"Perfect. I'm right there. Well, not exactly *there* since my vehicle didn't make it all the way up to the actual cabins."

Noah narrowed his gaze to squint through the blur of white that enveloped the Jeep. "Did you stall on the incline?"

"No." There was a detectable wary quality in the woman's answer. "I sort of drove it off the side of the road and now I'm completely stuck."

That information made Noah's pulse spike. How

hadn't he known that someone had been stranded at the entrance to their property? And for how many hours? This was something he'd be having a chat with his brothers about later on, that was certain. Maybe it was time to invest in some sort of surveillance, at the very least, a game camera.

"How long have you been stranded in your vehicle, ma'am?"

"Oh, I'm not still in the vehicle. I crashed it earlier in the day," she explained in a rush. "And crash is such a harsh term for what actually happened. More like I spun out, then slid into an embankment."

"You're not hurt?"

"No, I'm completely fine. Just looking for a tow."

As he edged closer, a fuzzy figure came into view, a woman in a bright green coat pacing the width of the road. Noah decelerated as he approached. When the woman turned, his foot jammed the brakes.

"Samantha?" he blurted into the phone.

Her pacing ceased, both feet planting beneath her. Samantha's head swiveled back and forth, disconcerted eyes roving in a panicked search. "Sir, I don't recall telling you my name."

"Samantha." Noah gave a little toot of his horn and the poor woman leapt in the air like a startled jackrabbit. She jerked her head around and her gaze caught Noah's through the windshield. He pointed to the phone near his ear. "It's me, Noah."

Confusion manipulated her features.

"I'm on the phone with you, Samantha. I'm the guy you called for a tow."

He figured that information would offer relief, not produce the near grimace that bent Samantha's lips instantly downward.

"Seriously?" She came up to the driver's side of the Jeep and peered through the glass, brow shaded against the relentlessly falling snow. "Oh, Noah. I really don't want to bother you with this."

"You're not bothering me," he replied. "But I am a bit bothered that you're standing out there in the cold when I'm in here with the heater running. Come around to the other side and get in."

She hesitated and Noah worried she might not take him up on the offer. But then her shoulders shook from a full-body shiver and Samantha scurried around the front end of the vehicle. Noah clicked off his cell phone and placed it into the breast pocket of his jacket, then reached across the cab to pop open the door.

With a massive exhale, Samantha climbed into the seat. Her hands were an icy blue—obviously chilled to the bone—and wet spots of melting snow darkened the fabric of her coat. Even her cheeks and lashes were dusted with iridescent flakes.

"Place your hands in front of the vent." Noah nudged his chin toward the dash as he cranked the dial for the heat. "Should thaw in no time."

Pinching the bridge of her nose with her fingers, Samantha groaned. "I thought the voice on the phone sounded familiar, but I *really* didn't want it to be you on the other end of the line."

Any confidence he had amassed plummeted within him, like a skydiver without a parachute. "Ouch. Not gonna lie, that hurts a little."

"I don't mean it like that," she retracted. "It's just —I already feel like I'm taking advantage of you by staying in the extra cabin free of charge. And I know you have so much on your plate right now. I imagine the last thing you want to do with your afternoon is pull my car out of the snow."

That couldn't be further from the truth. He'd volunteer for a root canal or willingly file his taxes— maybe even do both at once—if it meant spending more time getting to know Samantha.

"This is not an inconvenience. Promise."

She angled her head and shot him a look of pure doubt. "You were heading somewhere when I called."

He couldn't lie about that. "I was just driving into town to run an errand. But that can wait."

Samantha's head whipped from side to side, golden curls skimming along her slender shoulders. "No, no, no. My car can wait. Let's go run that errand and if we have time when we get back, we'll see about getting my car unstuck. First things first."

She had invited herself along—boldly, at that— and Noah couldn't mask his delight. "I just have to grab something at the hardware store," he said, then added, "but I was thinking about stopping for coffee on the way."

"Oh, Noah Jensen. You are speaking my language." She drew her hands to her mouth and cupped them there as she blew a warming breath. "I could use a good dose of caffeine right about now. Although I'm not sure it's possible to be more jittery than I already am."

"What's that about?" He guided the Jeep down the remaining stretch of road and flipped his blinker on to turn toward town. "The jitters?"

"I shouldn't admit this to you since I know you'll be responsible for the selection, but I really want this audition to work out for my parents. If Christmas wishes are a real thing, that's mine."

His heart sank a little with that information. He knew he was only one-fifth of the final vote, but he had influence all the same. And it would be a lie to say he didn't want Jack and Joan to secure the commercial spot. Granted, they were the only potential Santas he had met thus far, but in his eyes, they were as good as any.

Noah's pause must have come across as unease because Samantha backpedaled. "Of course, it's okay if they don't get it. It's not like it will financially ruin them or anything." She twisted her hands together in her lap like a knot. "I just think it could be an opportunity for healing. That's all."

Samantha volunteered no more than that, and Noah didn't press it. The remainder of the drive to the coffee shop was filled with comfortable silence, the soft rumbling of the tire tread and hum of the motor a relaxing lull. Out of his periphery, Noah caught little glimpses of Samantha, her mouth agape and eyes rounded in child-like awe. Over the winters, Noah had lost a bit of that curiosity and appreciation. Snow became an uncontrollable element to overcome, not something to wonder at.

Lifting a finger to the glass, Samantha pressed the window right where a snowflake had landed. "Isn't it incredible that they are all so different, so unique?" She kept the pad of her finger there as the flake slowly lost its crisp edges and began to pool. "Just like people. Uniquely and wonderfully made."

Noah didn't intend to let his gaze linger for as long as it did, so when Samantha stole a look and caught him, he offered a sheepish smile. His cheeks heated with an insecure flush, but the honest and beautiful grin she returned instantly set him at ease. Shifting his focus back onto the road, Noah cautioned himself not to get distracted. He had a destination, both today with his errand and tomorrow with the cabins. A detour—romantic or otherwise—was not in the plans.

Samantha Day was definitely not part of the plan.

CHAPTER 7

*S*amantha considered herself a coffeehouse connoisseur of sorts, but she had to admit that in her thirty-two years on the planet, she'd never come across the likes of one as peculiar as the cafe in Comfort Valley.

At first glance, *The Guzzler* was a timeworn, 1950s gas station, so when Noah pulled his Jeep off the road and into the gravelly lot pocked with holes, she figured it was to fill up the tank.

"We're going to fill up, alright. On piping hot coffee."

Samantha could only assume her face reflected her bewilderment.

"What?" Noah's mouth lifted into a dimpled grin. "You've never been served coffee out of a nozzle before?"

"I can't say I have," Samantha replied, still feeling like Noah might be yanking her chain.

He gradually angled the vehicle up to an open bay where a young man in a crisp, white uniform befitting an old timey gas station attendant flicked a wave in their direction. He stood under the covered awning and greeted them cheerfully. "Afternoon, Noah. What'll it be today? The usual?"

Rotating his wrist, Noah took a long look at his watch. "S'pose I should do decaf at this hour, Reggie. You know me. Caffeine keeps me up more effectively than a loud woodpecker on a metal roof."

The young man tugged a Styrofoam cup from a sleeve mounted on the pole and withdrew a gas nozzle from the pump. Gulping, Samantha very nearly choked on her own incredulity.

"Don't worry." Noah patted her knee in reassurance. "While most of *The Guzzler* is authentic with its original parts and historical charm, the gas pumps and holding tanks have been completely replaced."

"Only used for coffee," Reggie corroborated. "And creamer. You want a splash today, Noah?"

"Nope. Black is good."

Handing off the drink, Reggie stepped closer to the vehicle. "And what can I get you, Miss?"

Half joking, Samantha asked, "I don't suppose you have a pump that pours peppermint white mochas, do you?"

"The best I can do is medium roast with a splash of cream and one of these." He brandished a candy cane from his ticket pocket and passed it through the open window with a wink.

"That'll be just perfect." Samantha leaned across the front seat to take the striped candy, wedging herself directly within Noah's personal space. Notes of bergamot and pine hit her senses with dizzying force. She hadn't been close enough to Noah before to breathe in his scent, which was probably a good thing because his looks alone had been enough to render her nearly incoherent. Coupling this heady scent with his handsome appearance was a recipe for sheer delirium.

"That'll be eight-forty-two," Reggie announced as he handed the second drink to Noah.

Making a move for her backpack, Noah waved her off, hips lifting to slide his wallet from his back pocket. He counted out a handful of bills.

"Keep the change, buddy." Noah placed the coffee drink into the cup holder between them and offered Reggie a friendly wave. "See you next time."

Back on the two-lane highway, Samantha shook her head, still grinning from the experience.

"That's…not what I was expecting." She held the warm cup between her palms and enjoyed the way the steamy tendrils curled under her nose, tickling it like the wisp of a feather.

"You mean to tell me when I said we were going to grab coffee, you didn't assume it would be from a retrofitted gas station?"

Samantha appreciated the gentle ribbing and how effortless playful conversation seemed between them.

"You know, it might come as a shocker, but I sure didn't."

"Ah, you thought I would take you to one of those boring, sit-down sorts of places, didn't you?"

"How could I be so presumptuous?" she rallied. The first sip of the aromatic liquid burned the tip of her tongue, so she blew across the caramel-colored surface to lessen the scalding temperature.

"The only sit-down places we have in these parts are a little more formal. Like for lunch or dinner."

"Next time," Samantha said.

"Next time," Noah agreed, casting a quizzical look her way before directing his gaze back through the windshield, a tiny, but noticeable, grin fastened on his lips.

HAL'S HARDWARE DIDN'T HOUSE QUITE AS MANY surprises as the coffee shop, which was fine with Samantha. She was content to follow behind Noah as they traipsed up and down the aisles, cup of coffee in hand, a smile on her face. Noah seemed to know everyone and not just in a casual acquaintance sort of way. When they were standing in front of a plumbing display and Noah caught sight of an older gentleman, frail shoulders hunched and feet shuffling with the assistance of a shiny wooden cane, Noah inquired about the man's wife, Bessie. He even recalled the exact date of her recent medical procedure.

"Still waiting on the results, but we're hopeful," the man replied in a thin voice, shaky with emotion. "The good Lord has blessed us and I'm confident he'll continue to do so. The doctor said we should hear back by this Friday."

"I'll add it to my prayer list." Noah's large hand came down onto the elderly man's back in a heartfelt pat. "Take care of yourself, Thomas. And take care of that sweet Bessie of yours, too."

There were a handful more similar exchanges, and each one left Samantha filled with a profound respect she hadn't felt for anyone in a long while. Oliver was a respectable enough man, she supposed, but he wasn't the type to ask about others. He often spent so much time talking about himself, it left little opportunity for any other subject.

They were in the checkout line, new dryer vent in hand, when Noah's sudden shout made Samantha startle so much that the liquid in her cup sloshed all the way up to the rim, coming precariously close to spilling over and onto the concrete floor.

"Way to go, Caden Montgomery!" Noah hollered through hands cupped like a megaphone. A teenage boy with mousy brown, shoulder length hair capped in a knit beanie threw a fist in the air and pumped it enthusiastically.

"Nationals bound!" Caden chanted like a rally cry. The entire store erupted in applause, hoots and hollers swelling within the small warehouse space.

Even Samantha joined in, though she had no clue what they were celebrating.

"Caden's on the local high school snowboarding team and just placed first in state." Noah leaned closer to Samantha's ear. "That kid is going to be an Olympian one day. Mark my words."

"Do you know everyone in Comfort Valley?"

They stepped closer to the register as the line dwindled.

"Not everyone," Noah supplied humbly. "The Rockforts just had a baby boy last week and I haven't had a chance to meet him yet."

Samantha laughed. "A byproduct of working in the hospitality industry, I take it?"

Noah set the aluminum vent on the counter and smiled at the cashier. "A byproduct of being Andy Jensen's son and Paul Jensen's grandson. You could say the gift of gab has been passed down in our family tree, although it skipped a couple of branches. My older brother, Marty, isn't much of a talker."

"I wish I lived somewhere like this—where everyone knows one another."

"You live in a big city?"

"I work there. Downtown Sacramento. But I commute from the suburbs," Samantha explained. "I know my neighbors and most of the people who live on my street, but more in a neighborhood watch sort of capacity. I couldn't tell you their names, let alone the sports their children play."

"Well, a little of what's going on up here—

everyone knowing everything about everybody—has to do with the dismal amount of excitement we get in these parts. When something even remotely interesting happens, we all take note."

"Somehow, I don't think that's the true reason."

The cashier rattled off the total and slipped the part into a paper bag while Noah swiped his credit card through the machine.

Samantha faced him and said, "It's not just pleasantries on your part; it's genuine interest."

Noah shrugged. "I find people genuinely interesting." They took their purchase and walked toward the exit, side by side. Noah held the door open to usher Samantha through first. "I find *you* interesting."

Cold air hit Samantha's cheeks as a wet droplet from an icicle clinging to the gutter above slipped off and landed on her nose. She crinkled it and swiped the water off with her thumb.

"I wouldn't say I'm all that interesting." She rubbed her slick fingers together.

"Don't sell yourself short. You're very interesting. Your line of work alone is fascinating."

"A talent agent?" She followed Noah to the Jeep, surprised when he stayed close and opened her door first. She waited until he rounded the back end and situated himself in the driver's seat before continuing. "In reality, I guess it's my job to find interesting people."

"What led you to the industry?"

"You know, it just sort of came about. When I was

a kid, I was never the one to try out for the talent show. Instead, I would always encourage my friends to audition. I helped them find the things they were good at and urged them to show it off for all the world to see. I would get so much joy when someone I loved found their calling or discovered the things they were truly exceptional at. That passion naturally evolved into creating my own talent agency nearly a decade ago."

"You obviously have a knack for it if you've been at it for ten years already."

"I like to think I'm good at what I do," Samantha said. "What about you? Have you always wanted to be a handyman?"

Noah's gaze swung in her direction. "Try repeating that and see if you've already answered your own question," he teased, a glimmer of jovial mockery in his tone.

"I'm serious. Some people really love to fix things. A handyman is a noble profession."

"Okay, I'll give you that. It is," he offered, nodding along. "But no, I don't love to fix things. What I do love, however, is helping people."

That didn't surprise Samantha one bit. Even in their short time together, she got the distinct sense that Noah was the kind of man to put others first. He looked for ways to ease the burdens of others, and that was certainly admirable.

"What do you say we go get that car of yours unstuck?"

It was late, Samantha could tell by the way the winter sun slipped in the sky and dusk settled upon the mountain like a hazy blanket. Thankfully, the snow had ceased falling around an hour earlier, but she knew it had to be creeping up on dinnertime.

"Isn't it almost time for stew?" she asked.

"It is, but I'm sure Grandma Kitty will keep a bowl or two warm for us. They won't even notice we're gone."

Samantha would not take advantage of Noah's good nature more than she already had. She wasn't about to force him to miss dinner simply because she hadn't known how to drive in the snow. "You know what? My car can wait."

"We're expecting another dumping overnight. Come tomorrow, we might not even be able to find your little car beneath the pile of fresh powder."

"Then we'll have to find a way to mark it. Tag a nearby tree or something. I'm not about to miss Grandma Kitty's stew with the Santas."

CHAPTER 8

"I understand the whole 'getting into character thing'," Vera panted as she vigorously scrubbed the planked pine floor, "but is all of this soot really necessary?"

David commandeered the roll of paper towels from his wife and unwound several perforated sections. "Leave this to me, darling. Your only job right now is to take care of yourself and that sweet daughter of ours. Here, let me help you up."

The adoring look David gifted his wife would've made Noah roll his eyes in earlier years, but now the only sensation he felt as he viewed their endearing exchange was warmth spreading throughout his chest. Maybe even a small pang of jealousy, if he could be truly honest with himself.

Of the three Jensen men, David was the only one to marry and start a family. Not that Noah didn't want those things. He did. Yet, with every turn of the calendar year, his bachelor title seemed to stick more and more securely, until one day, he feared it would become completely permanent.

Samantha wasn't wrong when she'd suggested Noah knew everyone in Comfort Valley. That meant he also knew everyone in the dating pool. And, at his age, that pool had become as small as an inflatable tub. Were he ever to find love, he'd have to expand his radius and Noah just didn't have that kind of time.

"Let me help you with that, brother." He fired off a generous spray of all-purpose cleaner, dousing the ashy footprints sullying the entrance to the dining hall. If it hadn't created work for them—unnecessary work, at that—Noah would've appreciated Kris Kringle's painstaking process of tracking soot-stained boot prints wherever he walked. The twisty and meandering trail of coal was nearly a work of art. *Nearly*.

In fact, as Noah scanned the dining room, he felt as though he'd miraculously slipped into the North Pole itself. There was Sinterklaas at one table with his gold trimmed cape, pointed hat and armful of painted wooden shoes overflowing with trinkets and candies. Father and Mother Christmas—or Tammy and Carl, as Noah recalled from the reservation list— sat at a nearby table, dressed in decadent periwinkle brocade with thick, white fur trimming the edges of their elaborate garments. There was a distinct Victorian air about them, both fine and regal. Their sophisticated appearance reminded Noah of a collectable

Santa figurine his mother once kept on her mantel. It had a small lever underneath and when Noah would twist it, the sounds of *O' Holy Night* plucked out in tinny, metallic notes.

All Santa hopefuls had arrived for dinner on time, donning their best costumes and Santa Claus depictions. Noah couldn't be sure which potential actor it emanated from, but as he strolled about the room, the unmistakable saccharine aroma of cinnamon and sugar met his nose.

"Cookie cologne?" Noah muttered. "Is that even a thing?"

He pulled out a chair for his sister-in-law and took a seat next to her, leaving an empty one to his right. He assumed Samantha would share a table with her parents, but he gave credibility to the naïve bloom of hope within him and left the option open.

"I thought I smelled that, too," David agreed. "Vera mentioned it earlier, but I figured it was just her superhuman, pregnant senses at work again."

"No, St. Nicholas really does smell like snicker-doodles." Noah whirled around to see Samantha standing immediately behind him, a friendly smile fixed on her lips. "Mind if I join you?"

"Please. By all means." Gripping the back of the chair, Noah slid it out gently.

"Thank you. Looks like Mom and Dad made some friends and I honestly don't know how many more mall Santa stories I can live through."

"That's unfortunate because all we're talking

about at this table are our childhood memories of sitting on Santa's lap," David teased without missing a beat.

"I don't even *have* a lap anymore." Vera draped a hand across her round belly, then suddenly jerked. "Oh goodness! She kicked! That was a big one."

Vera's hand shot out in front of Noah and grasped onto Samantha's. Hauling it quickly toward her, she pressed it down on the curve of her stomach. "Do you feel that?"

He tried to keep his composure, but Samantha's slender arm pulled directly over his chest like a seat-belt made Noah's heart ram into his throat. He coughed quietly to clear it.

"There! She did it again!"

"I feel it!" Samantha shared Vera's enthusiasm. "I totally felt that kick."

Releasing her grip, Vera sighed deeply. "I tell you, this baby is going to be a gymnast, I'm sure of it. She does not stop moving," she groaned, shifting her weight in the solid chair. "And she's got Jensen DNA, which means once she's able to, I highly doubt she'll ever stop talking."

"As long as her first word is Dada," David chimed in.

"Oh, come on, we all know it'll be 'Uncle Noah'."

"I hear the word 'no' is a pretty common first word for babies, so you might not be too far off," Samantha chided.

Noah clutched his chest, feigning injury from the

insult. "Hey, now. But you know what? That's fine by me. I'll take whatever I can get."

As the four kept the lively conversation going, Grandma Kitty shuffled about the room, dismissing each table to the buffet line. Baskets of crumbly corn bread, bowls of garden mix salad dressed with balsamic vinaigrette, and several slow cookers of French venison stew lined a long, clothed table at the back of the room. Noah had offered to help his grandmother, but she liked to be the one to release the groups since she would customarily say a quick prayer of thanks with each table before guiding them toward their awaiting meal.

Once all of tonight's guests had the chance to visit the food station, Kitty finally came up to her grandsons' table.

"Saved the best for last?" David pushed back from his seat, eager to dig in.

"The last shall be first," she corrected. She waggled a crooked finger at her youngest grandchild. "You know that, David." Then she started right in on grace. "Thank you for this bounty before us. May it be blessed to our bodies. And please bless each and every one of our guests at the cabins this week."

They chorused in *amen* as chair legs scraped the floor.

Kitty snagged Samantha's hand and cupped it, momentarily holding her a few steps back from the group. "My Noah says you're a fan of venison stew. I must be honest, dear, it can be a bit gamey, just so you know."

"I know it can be, but I really do like it. My dad and brother used to hunt every season back when we were kids, so I think there's a bit of nostalgia there. In fact, my parents still have the beautiful eight-point buck Seth shot on his tenth birthday. It's mounted right above their fireplace. I'm pretty sure they're the only Mr. and Mrs. Claus to have an actual deer head hanging on their wall."

"Nothing wrong with that. We can all separate fact from fiction around here," Kitty assured.

"Really?" Pulling a face, David made a sweeping motion with his arms at the display of costumed couples gathered within the room. "I do believe the fact that we're currently surrounded by a dozen Santas flies in the face of that."

"I think it's fun that everyone is in character even though the auditions don't start until tomorrow," Vera challenged. She picked up a salad plate from the towering stack and passed one off to her husband. "These cabins haven't seen this much magic in years."

"I heard a little something about that," Samantha noted. "The magic."

"You have?" Noah lifted the lid to one of the crock pots and collected the ladle from the spoon rest nearby. The hearty, comforting aroma of his grandmother's famous stew made his taste buds instantly tingle.

"My ex-husband mentioned it as I was leaving the office yesterday."

He knew he didn't have any right to the information, but it still set Noah off-kilter. Samantha had not only been married before, but evidently she currently worked with her ex, a scenario Noah could only imagine was a complicated one. Just that one short sentence housed a wealth of information.

"He used to visit the cabins as a child and said something about them being enchanted."

"He'd be right about that." Grandma Kitty stole the ladle from Noah's hand and dipped it back into the stew to scoop out a hearty portion. "Don't be shy, Noah. I made enough to feed an army. You too, Samantha."

Holding her dish steady, Samantha allowed Kitty to fill her soup bowl to capacity.

"Decades ago, these cabins used to be the talk of the town. Especially at Christmastime." Even though she wasn't eating, Kitty joined her grandchildren back at their table, depositing herself right next to Samantha. "It was my husband, Paul, who first had the idea to really play things up during the holidays. We would hire a Santa for the entire month of December and he would meet with the children staying here to listen to their Christmas wishes. Then Paul would spend his days in the woodshop behind the cottages, making the toys on their wish lists for Santa to deliver to their rooms on Christmas morning."

"I remember that," David said around a mouthful

of cornbread. "Vaguely, but I remember Dad and Gramps tinkering around in the shed back when we were little. I think I still have the wooden train set I asked Santa for when I was five."

"I'm sure you do." There was a thoughtful gleam in Kitty's eye. "Over the years, the requests got more and more complex, you know? Things like video games and electronics. Paul couldn't really make those and rather than deal with the few complaints we would receive here and there about his simple toys, he decided to scrap the modest operation altogether."

"He stopped making Christmas toys because kids got too greedy?" Samantha's voice was almost pained.

"Kids didn't get greedy," Kitty contested. "They just didn't know any better. It's completely normal to want the next big thing, and Paul's humble creations couldn't compete. And when Sierra Elevations Resort and Spa opened up down the highway, many of our regulars started filtering their way. Much like my husband's crafted toys, we soon realized our little mountain cabins couldn't compete, either."

"I'm so sorry to hear that." Samantha covered Kitty's hand with her palm.

"It's alright, dear. Maybe we should have evolved with the times, but I've always held out hope that nostalgia was just as important as innovation. For some folks, at least."

Noah wasn't sure he'd ever heard the timeline of their cabins told in such a way. The ache in his chest caught him by surprise, but the empathy in Samantha's gaze as she comforted his precious grandmother made his eyes mist over. He swallowed past the lump crowding his throat.

"That's the reason for the commercial," Samantha surmised. "To tap into the nostalgia inherent in the Christmas season."

"Exactly," Kitty conferred. "It's not likely to ramp up business overnight, but our dream is that someone will see it and remember coming here as a child. Maybe they'll even want their own children to experience Christmas at the cabins. One can only hope."

CHAPTER 9

*S*amantha hadn't slept well, and it had nothing to do with the unfamiliarity of her surroundings or the bed that differed from her own. No, all the comforts of Cabin #8 should have ushered in a peaceful night's sleep. It was her brain that wouldn't let her find rest despite the plush mattress beneath her and the fluffy pillows cradling her troubled head.

The story Kitty had shared over dinner upset her. She knew those children weren't to blame for the financial downfall of the cabins. It was silly to think that. It wasn't even the competing resort that caused the dire situation. Kitty was right—time ushered in change. More often than not, that change was welcome.

But simplicity wasn't a bad thing. Samantha knew that.

She recalled her time volunteering at the children's hospital years earlier. Her parents had a long-standing contract with the local hospital and served as their designated Santa year after year, visiting children who often didn't have the fortune of wishing for anything other than health, strength, and maybe even just one more Christmas.

At the time, Samantha was a grumbly teenager, outfitted in an elf costume her parents practically forced her to wear. Her younger brother, Seth, was relentless in his teasing every time she would squeeze into the vivid green tights and tunic, complete with floppy felt cap that always dangled right between her eyes. She hated his constant goading, up until the day Seth was the boy resting in the hospital bed. She would wear that silly costume every season for the remainder of her years just to be on the receiving end of his teasing one more time.

It had consistently surprised her how often a child would ask Santa for a gift for their sibling, their friend, or even the patient in the room down the hall. They understood the true meaning of Christmas: the precious gift of sacrifice and love.

Other than the hospital, Samantha couldn't recall experiencing that pure, selfless holiday spirit anywhere else.

But she could sense it here at the Cedar Crest Cabins. She could feel that generosity embodied in the Jensen family and knew there had to be a way to tap into it. A way to let everyone else in on this charming, good place.

Could a commercial do that? Maybe, but Samantha was well aware a thirty-second blip on a television screen was hardly enough time to convince someone to buy a two-dollar toothbrush, let alone fork over several hundred dollars, schedule time off of work, and travel to a faraway mountain destination.

There had to be another strategy, but her brainstorming efforts came up empty.

Rolling over, Samantha gathered the heavy quilt into her grip, collecting the fabric under her chin to snuggle beneath the warmth trapped there. Snow fell in lazy, scattered flakes just outside the window. Were she back at home, Samantha would've hit the snooze button on her alarm to steal a few more moments of slumber, but the busy day that awaited her here caused a bubble of anticipation to swell within her.

There was the yummy promise of homemade cinnamon rolls for breakfast, the hope of resurrecting her car from its snowy encampment, and the excitement of her parents' audition that afternoon.

And there was Noah.

Each time her thoughts traveled to him, Samantha's stomach tumbled, like cresting the apex of an amusement park rollercoaster. She had assumed this visceral—and admittedly, superficial—reaction would've subsided once she got to know him a little better. That was often the case with good-looking men. They knew the effect their appearance had on women and they manipulated that to their advantage. But somehow, Samantha got the sense Noah didn't have a clue just how handsome he was. That unawareness was undeniably attractive in and of itself.

Inhaling fully, Samantha sat up and brought her arms over her head, clasping her hands to stretch toward the ceiling. The crisp, earthy scent of pine spread over her senses. It didn't even bother her that the Christmas tree was still bare. It was glorious all the same with its thick, branching layers and perfectly tapered point, just waiting to be decked with a star or an angel. She could see the potential in it—what it could become.

She also saw the potential in the cabins. It was there, as natural and lovely as that evergreen.

Dressing quickly in fitted jeans, a slouchy, burgundy cowl-neck sweater, and a pair of snow boots lined with soft fur, Samantha gave herself a once over in the mirror before gathering her backpack to head to the adjacent cabin. Her father's rich voice reached her ears even before her mother opened the door to welcome her in.

"He's been reciting his lines since sunup," Joan explained, a twinge of annoyance infiltrating her characteristically sweet voice. "All the while, I've been trying to figure out what to do with this ghastly mop of hair."

"I can help with that. Did you happen to bring a curling iron?" Samantha scooted into the cabin and closed the door gently behind her.

"I did. And about a thousand bobby pins. But I tell you, Sam, I'm dreadfully out of practice. I forgot how much time it takes to get into character." Joan cast a look toward her husband. "Unlike your father who wakes up each morning looking like Santa's doppelgänger."

"He does have that going for him." Samantha joined her mother in the small bathroom. She gathered a comb from the ledge of the pedestal sink and plugged the iron into the wall to heat. "But we'll have you looking like his North Pole partner in crime in no time."

"I'm just not sure about this whole thing," Joan confided on a resigned breath.

"Have some faith, Mom. I'm confident we can transform you into a believable Mrs. Claus, just like we used to."

"That's not exactly what I'm talking about." Seating herself on a stool in front of the mirror, Joan connected gazes with her daughter's reflection.

"What do you mean?"

Joan sectioned off a portion of her hair between two fingers. Samantha took hold of it, coiling it around the curling iron, eyes fastened on her mother's. "Sam, have you read the script?"

Almost ashamed to admit it, Samantha spoke a

quiet, "No. I haven't had the chance. Not yet, at least. But I will."

The entire reason she came to the cabins was to help prepare her mom and dad for their big audition. How had she not even taken the time to go over the script first?

"Maybe you should take a peek at it," Joan said, shrugging back when the hot iron came dangerously close to her ear. "Better yet, let Dad fill you in. Jack, sweetie? Can you come in here for a moment?"

Jack's commanding presence at Samantha's back made her do a double take. He was Santa Claus in the flesh, from the velvety red cap atop his head to his black leather boots strapped on his large feet. Even the sparkle in his eye when he glimpsed his beloved wife and daughter matched the famed man in red.

"Mrs. Claus, you beckoned?"

"As you can clearly see, I'm not quite Mrs. Claus yet. Still just plain ol' Joan." She shook her head, tugging Samantha's hand and the iron with it.

"Hold still, Mom. I really don't want to burn you."

"Alright, alright." Joan made a harrumph sound. "Jack, would you mind reciting a few of your lines for our daughter? It seems she hasn't familiarized herself with the script just yet."

Jack scanned the pack of stapled papers in his hand. "Do you want me to start at the part where I say, *'Forget the Bahamas, I spend my off season at Cedar Crest*

Cabins!'? Or the part where I ask to be left margaritas and nachos instead of cookies and milk?"

"Give that to me." Samantha hurled the curling iron into the empty sink basin and ripped the sheets of paper from the father's hands. Skimming over the dialogue, her stomach soured, each line worse than the previous one. "Oh my goodness. This is truly awful."

"Awful is such a strong word," Jack defended.

"I know. And I'm concerned it's not even strong enough for what this is." Samantha's free hand went to her forehead and she let out a groan of disbelief. "I'm so, so sorry. I should have done more research before dragging you both here for something this amateurish. Obviously, it's not quite the magical opportunity I thought it to be."

"It's not *all* bad. There is a scene involving a bikini-clad Mrs. Claus and palm fronds."

"Are you serious?" Samantha frantically rifled through the pages, fanning them out like a children's flipbook.

"No," Jack said with a hearty laugh. "I'm teasing about that. But maybe we can ask if they're willing to embellish a little."

Rolling up the papers like a newspaper, Samantha swatted her father squarely in the chest. "Ha, *ha*," she enunciated in annoyance. "In all seriousness, do you mind taking over here for a bit with curling duties? I'm going to see what I can do about this."

"Not sure there's much to be done. I saw the

camera crew rolling in this morning on my way to the dining hall for breakfast. They were already setting things up when I left."

"You've already had breakfast?" Samantha asked, wondering where the morning had gone. "Was Noah there?"

"He was. We chatted for a bit, but he was on his way to tow someone out of a ditch with his Jeep."

Samantha clenched her molars together. "He was on his way to tow my car?"

"You know what? That hadn't occurred to me, but I suppose there's a very good chance it could be yours. Makes the most sense now, doesn't it?"

"Dad, where are your truck keys?"

"On the nightstand." Jack collected the discarded curling iron and started to loop it around a lock of Joan's hair.

"Do you mind if I borrow it?"

"Only if you promise to stay on the road this time. Not sure Noah's Jeep has the power to haul that beast of an automobile out of the snow."

"Very funny, Dad," Samantha chided. "I'll be back soon. Is it okay if I take the script with me?"

"Sure thing. I've already got most of it committed to memory."

Samantha shook her head, still stunned by the disappointing discovery. "Hard to forget something this terrible."

"Isn't that a form of marketing? To create something just controversial enough that it sticks with the viewer?"

"If I have my way, this will not stick at all."

Her parents deserved better. The cabins deserved better. And whoever came up with this piece of drivel? Well, Samantha was going to see that they got exactly what they deserved.

CHAPTER 10

The bulky gloves made it difficult to grip firmly onto the chains, but Noah knew better than to take them off. With temperatures this cold, his fingers would numb into ten icicles, rendering them totally useless. After spending a good hour digging Samantha's vehicle out from beneath a solidly packed hunk of snow, he was so close to securing her car to his Jeep. Just one more chain and it would be good to haul out.

"This is terrible!"

He wasn't surprised to hear her voice. After all, when he saw Jack's truck rumbling down the driveway at a snail's pace, he assumed it was Samantha at the helm. She was nothing but overly cautious as the large vehicle crawled closer, and Noah appreciated that. It had only taken one unintended off-roading incident to turn her into an adept mountain driver, and that was better than most.

"Terrible?" Noah asked when Samantha jumped down from the cab of the truck, arms waving as though directing an incoming plane. "I thought you'd be happy to finally get your car out of the snow."

"Not the car." She shook her head. "Thank you for that." She flapped a handful of papers in the air. "This! This is terrible!"

"What's that?" Crouched down, Noah secured the last chain to the hitch and swiped his gloves together, shaking off the snow. He pressed up to his feet with a grunt.

"The script for the commercial." Coming closer to the connected cars, Samantha lowered her voice from an all out yell to a less agitated tone. "Please, *please* tell me you didn't write this."

"I didn't write that. In fact, I haven't even read it."

"Is this some sort of joke?"

"Seeing that I don't even know what's on those pages, I don't think I can confidently answer that."

Pressing the papers to his stomach, Samantha stepped back and crossed her arms over her chest. "Read it. You don't even have to read all of it. The first few lines set the tone for the entire atrocity."

Giving the script a furtive once over, Noah couldn't suppress the snicker that slipped between his lips.

"You think it's funny?"

"I mean,"—he shrugged—"it is. Sort of."

Samantha puffed a breath of pure irritation that suspended in a wispy cloud in front of her mouth.

Her nose was red and her cheeks frosted with a chilled pink, but her eyes were ablaze with a heated irritation Noah could feel like a presence, even at the distance of several feet.

"I know my parents didn't sign up for some ridiculous comedy sketch when they came here. And I doubt the others did, either. If this is your idea of—"

"Like I said, this isn't my idea. The commercial, yes. That part was mine. But I didn't have a hand in writing this script. That's all the screenwriter."

Snatching the papers back, Samantha shoved the packet under her arm. "But you hired the screenwriter."

"I didn't hire him. My brother, Marty, did."

"You have another brother?" She said it accusingly, like she should have been privy to that information, much the way Noah had felt taken aback when she'd mentioned her ex-husband the night before.

"Yes, I have another brother. And Marty is…" Noah paused, taking purposeful time to select his words. "Marty does things a little differently than the rest of us do."

"Seems to me like this is a case where the right hand doesn't know what the left is doing."

"That's fair. Honestly, none of us really know what we're doing, if that hasn't been made obvious yet."

Features softening and stance less squared, Samantha's mouth pressed into a line. "That's not what I meant—"

"It's true. My dad and grandpa were the ones running the show around here. We're just the reserves, scrambling to recreate something they had the real vision for."

"What can we do about this?" Glancing toward the script, Samantha lifted her eyes to meet Noah's. "I mean, we obviously can't proceed with this."

"I'll have a chat with Marty, but I do know the guy he hired for the commercial 'owed him a favor'." Noah made air quotes around the words. "That's how Marty's world works. He cashes in on debts and racks up new ones. I probably never should've let him run with it, but as you can see, we're working with a skeleton crew around here and we're all trying our best."

"I find it hard to believe this script is anyone's best."

"When you're asking people to work for free, sometimes you can't be too picky."

Samantha's mouth dropped open. "Your production team is working for free?"

"That's what Marty negotiated. We earmarked most of our finances to pay the talent and that left little in the bank to work with for the other stuff."

"Noah, you do realize this isn't the way the industry works, right?"

"I really have no clue how the industry works. But I agree, that right there isn't any sort of award-winning script." He nudged his chin toward the papers under her arm. "Do you have a better idea?"

"I think I just might. Where is your brother?"

NOAH COULDN'T SAY HE LOVED THE THOUGHT OF introducing Samantha to Marty—not when she clearly had a bone to pick with him—but he couldn't see a way around it. Something needed to be done about the script; he agreed with her on that. But changing things up this late in the game would lengthen their entire production calendar, and that just wasn't feasible. Each extra day they housed their guests free of charge was another day in the red for the Cedar Crest Cabins.

After pulling her car free and tucking it away in a proper parking space near the lodging facilities, Noah took a long, hot shower, hoping the water would wash away the apprehension vice-gripping his chest.

The last thing he wanted was a confrontation with Marty. Over the years, he had learned to work with his older brother—how to read him and react accordingly. If Samantha came in guns blazing like she had when she'd confronted Noah on the road, things would go south quickly. He knew that.

They had halted auditions, citing unfavorable lighting as the reason for the holdup. Most guests seemed agreeable with the sudden change in plans, though Noah noted a few grumbles here and there. Those quickly quieted when his mother announced an afternoon of free hot chocolate and carols around the piano in the dining hall.

These people loved Christmas, every last one of them. They loved it the way bears loved honey. Sure, Noah favored Jack and Joan merely because they were Samantha's parents, but the reality was, every Santa on the property was more than qualified for their commercial. Especially considering this particular commercial wasn't even worthy of airing on a cable access channel.

Picking up his phone, Noah began to text Marty just as a knock sounded on his door. Noah got little foot traffic. His living quarters were just above the dining hall and only accessible via an outside staircase that was typically layered with several inches of snow. Only a family member would know his whereabouts, so when he opened the door and saw Marty's face— features pulled tight in apparent frustration—Noah just nodded knowingly.

"Hey, brother. I was about to text you."

"Already got the other three you sent." Marty lumbered past, making a beeline for the kitchenette near the back of the studio apartment.

"Come on in," Noah welcomed, albeit facetiously, as he held out an ushering hand. "You know, when someone texts you, the polite thing to do is to text them back."

"We're not firing Donnie." Marty took a tumbler from the cabinet and then stretched taller to pull down a bottle of amber-colored liquid from the uppermost shelf. He poured a healthy glug and brought the glass to his lips. "That's not even an option."

"I'm not suggesting we fire him." Intercepting the carafe before Marty had a chance to top off his cup, Noah placed the libation back into the cupboard and closed the door. For goodness' sake, it wasn't even noon. "I just think we should be open to going another direction with the tone of it all. Have you actually read it?"

"I have." Marty balled up a fist and thrust it against his chest as he cleared his throat from the burn. "It's fine."

"But it's not really. We're a winter travel destination. The way the script reads, it sounds like we're some beach resort."

"Donnie says it's what sells."

"That might be true of another market, but definitely not ours. We're going to have to sell slushy drinks with fancy little umbrellas and dig a pool out back if that's the sort of clientele we want to attract."

"He suggested we do that."

Noah's jaw unhinged. "I was kidding."

He should've seen it coming, but when Marty slammed his glass onto the counter, sending a spray of liquid from the cup, he still jumped.

"You wanted me to be a part of this process, even though I had no interest from the beginning. And now you're going to criticize me for trying to help?" Lifting two hands in front of his chest, Marty waved them and took a step back. "Nope. I don't think so. I'm done. The rest of you are on your own."

"And how's that any different from usual?" The moment the words escaped his mouth, Noah regretted uttering them.

"You know, I've spent my entire life trying and failing to live up to the Jensen name." Marty moved angrily forward and jammed a pointed index finger into Noah's chest. "I'm *done*. You want to carry on the tradition of these cabins? By all means, go for it. But don't include me in your efforts anymore. This place is a sinking ship and it's well past time I got off."

CHAPTER 11

"*A*nd a partridge in a pear tree!"

The last piano note rang out, the collection of voices holding a beat longer. Samantha had forgotten what a good carol could do for the soul. Her earlier agitation all but subsided with each melody, every carol a gentle reminder of Christmas-time peace, goodwill, and tradition.

It had been Samantha's first time meeting Noah's mother, and it was a lovely introduction at that. When Samantha had walked into the room, Audrey waved her over and slid on the long piano bench, making room for Samantha to perch on the edge next to her. She had asked if Samantha would turn the pages of sheet music, and Samantha gladly agreed to help. It was the very best seat in the hall with guests surrounding the baby grand, their voices swelling like harmonious waves around them. Some leaned close, propping their elbows on the piano while others kept time with clapping hands or stomping feet.

Audrey's fingers hovered over the keys, readying to tickle them with the familiar notes of another holiday song. "Up for one more?" she asked the crowd. She lifted a hand and rifled through the pages on the stand.

"I need a moment after that one," Jack admitted, palm to his chest as he pretended to wheeze. "I forgot how much breath it takes to get through those twelve days!"

"Then it sounds like the perfect time to break for some hot cocoa."

When Samantha arrived for the carols an hour earlier, the first thing she had glimpsed was the hot chocolate bar at the back of the room. It hadn't been there the night before when they'd gathered for dinner. She would have noticed the charming display. Glass jars filled with puffy marshmallows of varying sizes, twisted candy cane sticks, and bricks of chocolate sat next to a metal carafe of hot water, all displayed on a white tablecloth covered in embroidered, delicate holly berries. It looked like a festive beverage station that belonged at a wedding or fancy corporate function, and Samantha made a mental note to recreate a similar one for their company's holiday party later that month.

"What can I get you, sweetie?" Jack asked Samantha when it was their turn in line. He took a packet of hot chocolate mix and ripped off the top before withdrawing a red mug from the towering stack of mismatched cups.

"Just a hot chocolate with a few marshmallows. Thanks, Dad."

"Coming right up."

Jack was always one to serve others. When Samantha was a little girl, her father couldn't make a trip through their galley kitchen without asking if anyone wanted anything. He consistently thought of others' needs before his own. To this day, Samantha couldn't understand how she had ended up with a man like Oliver—one who didn't know the meaning of the word service—given her father had set such a selfless example for their family.

"Careful, it's hot," Jack cautioned as he handed off the steaming mug. "Although I suppose it would just be called 'chocolate' if it wasn't."

Gathering the warm cup in her hands, Samantha laughed, but that lightheartedness quickly turned sour. She needed to talk with her parents about the commercial. She wasn't sure how much longer she could stall.

"Hey, can I borrow you for a second?" The fingers grazing her elbow made her jolt, her heart kicking up in tempo. Samantha turned around and her gaze met Noah's.

"Hi." She couldn't mask the flustered quality in her voice. "Sure. Of course. We can talk." Stepping backward, Samantha offered her father an apologetic look. "I'll just be a minute, Dad."

"Take all the time you need. I'm going to check in on your mother and see if she's almost done with her hair. I'm worried she's singed it all off by now."

Noah's expression remained neutral as they walked to the corner of the room and out of earshot.

"Is everything okay?" Samantha lifted her mug closer to her lips and blew across the top of it. Slowly, she pulled in a cooled sip and held it in her mouth.

"The crew just left."

Choking on the hot chocolate, Samantha shook her head and swallowed. "Crew? The camera crew?"

"The entire production team. And Marty along with them."

Samantha coughed loudly to clear her throat once more. Her throat burned with the effort. "They all left," she said as a statement, as though repeating it would somehow help to make sense of the situation they were suddenly thrust into.

"Yep. They *all* left." Noah's jaw twitched. "And now I have a dozen Santas, no commercial script, and no camera crew. I'm planning to break the bad news to everyone at dinner this evening, but I wanted to give you a heads up first."

Samantha nodded. "Thank you for that. I appreciate it."

Rubbing the back of his neck, Noah gave a helpless shrug. "I guess it's now abundantly clear that my talent isn't resurrecting failed businesses."

"Noah, don't sell yourself so short. Look around you. You managed to gather this many potential candidates during their busiest time of year. That's no small feat."

"I think the promise of a paycheck did that," he conceded. "I'm going to give everyone the option to stay the full week since that's what we offered from the beginning, but I have a feeling most will want to leave sooner rather than later to move onto bigger and better things."

Samantha understood that. "Thank you for telling me, Noah." She placed her hand on his arm, but then yanked it back.

"Of course." His eyes flitted down to where she had briefly touched him, then his gaze traveled back up to hers, expression pained. "I just wanted to make sure you knew so I had the chance to say goodbye before you headed out."

Pulling her chin back, Samantha cocked her head and challenged Noah with a stare. "Oh, I don't plan to leave."

Eyes foggy with confusion, he narrowed them. "What?"

"I took vacation time for this, Noah. I intend on using it." Then, smirking behind her mug, she added, "And I still have a tree to decorate."

"It's so good to hear your voice, Trish."

Samantha toed off her boots, one by one, and then flopped onto the mattress. It started to snow more heavily that afternoon, but within the confines of the cabin, she didn't mind the impending storm one bit. If anything, it only added to that sought after White Christmas feel.

"Hopefully you'll be hearing my voice through more than just your phone very soon," Trish Whitley said excitedly. "They just announced that my first Christmas single should hit the airwaves early next week! I'm still pinching myself, Sam. Feels like a dream!"

That was just the sort of uplifting news Samantha needed. Everything else about the day led to a steady decline in her typically joyful spirit.

"That's wonderful news, Trish! I'm truly so happy for you. No one deserves this success more than you."

"That's debatable, but thank you, friend. It's fair to say I wouldn't be where I am without you," Trish said. "So, tell me a little more about where *you* are right now. Oliver said you went on some trip up to the mountains?"

"Working vacation, actually. But everything has suddenly fizzled." Winding a loose thread from the wool blanket around her finger, Samantha mindlessly fiddled with the yarn. "It was supposed to be a commercial audition for my parents. But I didn't do my due diligence and it's all sort of a mess now. A big one."

"That's too bad. You deserve a break more than anyone I know. Sorry the place ended up being a bust."

"The place isn't a bust, just the project. In fact, the place is great. Really great. We're staying in these cute little log cabins and each one has its own Christmas tree. Everything feels so homey and inviting. And the family that runs it—they're wonderful, Trish. So kind and caring. Noah's doing his best to keep the cabin's legacy running—"

"Ah, I think I'm understanding things now."

"Understand what?"

"This Noah—does he happen to be around your age?"

Samantha hadn't asked his age, but figured they were within a few years of one another. "I don't know. I suppose so."

"And is he handsome?"

"Sure. Some might consider him handsome."

Trish snickered through the line. "So is the place really great, or is this Noah character really great?"

Samantha's stomach tumbled like a washer full of sodden towels. "Both are great. But that's beside the point."

"Is it, though?" Trish wasn't letting up, but Samantha didn't expect any less from her friend. Trish's tenacity was an enormous factor in her success; Samantha knew that. "Weren't you just saying the last time we went to lunch that you were ready to put your heart back on the market? That you wasted too much time moping around after your split from Oliver. That you were ready for love again?"

"I might've said that. But that's neither here nor there. As I said earlier, this is a working vacation."

"And in your words, it completely fizzled. Sounds like you can officially drop the 'working' part of it and focus on the enjoying part. And maybe this Noah guy can help you out a little in that department."

inding the box of ornaments in the attic was worth the lungful of dust. Noah couldn't stop thinking about Samantha's sad, unornamented tree and how bare it must look and feel in her cabin. And now that she was planning to stay the full week, Noah moved locating the decorations to the top of his list. It wasn't officially the Christmas season until all the trees were trimmed and stockings hung.

Things were quiet around the property that evening. In all, four couples opted to leave once they heard the disappointing news about the failed commercial endeavor. It didn't help that a hefty storm was on the horizon, either. The mass Santa exit wasn't a big surprise to Noah, but his heart sank with each goodbye. It felt like a wasted opportunity and he was painfully aware there wasn't much he could do about it. They were without a camera crew, a promotional idea, or any real plan to speak of. He'd have to go back to the drawing board eventually, but for tonight, his only plan was to deliver this box of ornaments to Samantha.

With the cardboard box in his grip, Noah trekked down the hill toward cabin eight. From the small front window, he could see a fire flickering in the hearth, its warm amber hue climbing the log walls in a dance of light and shadow. He was glad Samantha made herself at home and hadn't left with the rest of them. The thought of spending a few more days with her was a pleasant one. But she wasn't here to fraternize with Noah. He knew that. She was on vacation, and other than dropping off the necessary ornaments, Noah pledged to stay out of her hair. He'd created enough trouble in her world already.

Moving the box to his hip so he could lift a fist to the door, Noah knocked three quick times in a row.

"Coming!" Samantha called out from the other side. He heard the lock turn over before the door swung open on its hinges. "Oh, hey, Noah. What's up?"

She had a towel twisted around her hair and wore an oversized gray sweatshirt that had a snowman appliqué on the chest, paired with black leggings tucked into fuzzy sheepskin boots. Even with her face free of any detectable makeup, she was so naturally beautiful that Noah's breath caught.

"Hey. I…uh…I just wanted to bring these over." He rotated the box so the side that had ***decorations*** written in permanent marker faced her. "I hope it's not too late to stop by."

"Not too late at all. I was just winding down my evening."

She unbound her hair from the towel and placed the terrycloth onto an empty hook on the coat rack near the door. Damp blonde curls tumbled over her shoulders. Noah tried not to gape, but she looked like she stepped right out of a shampoo commercial and the hint of hibiscus that wafted toward him only added to that.

"Would you like to come in?"

"Not if you're getting ready for bed. I won't keep you." It wasn't even eight o'clock, but the day had been a long one and Noah didn't blame Samantha if she hoped to turn in early.

"I'm not going to bed yet. Just unwinding. Come on in."

He gave her a funny look. "What's unwinding involve?" Noah was an *asleep within ten seconds of hitting the pillow* sort of guy. He hadn't realized there was a process to ending one's day.

"Just relaxing. Having a glass of wine and enjoying the fire." She welcomed him in and then sat on the loveseat, legs tucked up beneath her. An empty glass rested next to a slender bottle on the coffee table and she bent forward to reach for it. "Can I pour you one?"

"Sure. Yeah, I'll have a cup." Noah lowered into the leather chair across from her.

"You mean a glass?" she corrected with a tiny grin. "I've never heard anyone ask for a cup of wine. But then again, you do get your coffee out of a pump, so maybe you all do things a little differently around here." The fluttery wink tacked on at the end of her words brought levity to the increasingly embarrassing interaction.

"I should be honest; I'm not much of a wine drinker."

Samantha halted. "I can get you something else. Maybe a hot chocolate? Although I suppose you probably had your fill this afternoon. Coffee?"

"No, I'll try the wine," Noah answered. "It's good for me to step out of my comfort zone every once in a while, right?"

Taking the neck of the bottle into her grip, Samantha poured a half-glass of deep red liquid. She swirled it around a few times, making the wine paint the crystal with opaque streaks. "If you're not a big wine guy, this might have too much bite for you. It's a barbera, so it's pretty tart. It's from a little winery in the foothills just up the road from where I live. I bought an entire case the last time I visited; I just love it so much."

"Well then, with a recommendation like that, I have to try it." Swinging the glass up to his lips, Noah pulled in a full mouthful. Instantly, his tongue soured at the back near his throat and his eyes filled with stinging tears. "Oh! You're not kidding. That is bitter. You sure that bottle's still good?"

"It's perfect." Samantha's sip was much slower as she savored it behind her lips. "Thank you for bringing the decorations over. You really didn't need to do that."

"Sure, I did." Noah tried another swig, hoping the second go-around would be less acidic, but no such luck. He abandoned his glass to the table and looked directly at Samantha. "A properly decorated tree is an absolute must here at Cedar Crest Cabins."

"It's my favorite part." She glanced at him, a wistful gleam sparkling her emerald eyes. "The tree decorating. I know the actual hunt for the perfect tree is the best part for some, but I've found you can dress up any tree to make it feel Christmassy. Even a spindly Charlie Brown one."

"That seems to be a common theme for you. The ability to bring out the beauty in everything."

Noah thought he caught a blush creep across her cheeks, but he attributed that to the wine.

"That's generous of you to say. I just like to help things reach their potential. Sometimes that's a person. Sometimes it's a tree. I don't discriminate."

He wanted to note that he felt like the best version of himself when he was around her, but the statement was too forward for their casual conversation. Not that the next words to leave his mouth were any less direct.

"So, did I hear you right when you said you have an ex-husband?"

"You did," Samantha willingly offered before

Noah had a chance to recoil from his bold question. "Oliver. We work together."

"And how's that? Working with your ex?" He pondered trying another taste of the wine, but he just couldn't do it.

"Better than being married. We've always worked well together." Suspending her glass in front of her pursed lips, she added, "I think that was the entire problem. I assumed since we were such great partners in the work realm, it would transfer to success in a romantic relationship. Considering we're divorced, it's fair to say I was completely wrong about that."

"I'm so sorry." Noah brought his ankle up to his knee and loosely crossed his legs. He fiddled with the laces on his rugged boot. "I can imagine that must have been difficult."

"Being married to a man who only thinks of himself is difficult; there's no denying that."

Noah couldn't imagine being with a woman like Samantha and thinking of anything *but* her. When he glimpsed the dejected look on her face, he almost spoke the thought in audible words. He wanted to tell her he hadn't stopped thinking of her since she'd checked into the cabins. Unlike his earlier comment, he kept those revealing musings to himself.

"What about you?" she continued. "Any engagements or marriages?"

"I'm a perpetual bachelor, it seems. I dated a little in the past, but I've stopped actively searching for love and just keep my fingers crossed, hoping that it finds me instead."

"That's one method. Just hope and pray that a spouse will arrive at your front door," Samantha teased.

"It worked for my grandpa."

Her eyes went wide.

"If you can believe it, my grandmother's car stalled right out there on that driveway some fifty-odd years ago. They never could get it restarted. She essentially stopped at Cedar Crest Cabins and never left. How's that for a love story, huh?"

Samantha's eyes rounded even more completely and as Noah replayed his words in his head, he realized how direct all of that information must have come across.

"Bet you're glad we got that car of yours up and running again," he added lightheartedly.

Spinning the long stem of her glass between her fingers, she said, "I don't know. This seems like a pretty great place to land."

Eyes lifting, Samantha's open gaze met Noah's. A charge as strong as electricity passed between them. For a moment, her eyes seem to beckon him to make some sort of move. Heart thrumming, he wondered if he was reading it all wrong. To misunderstand things and fail would be detrimental at this point. He'd already messed things up so badly. But there was a shred of hope he couldn't ignore, and when Samantha moved to place her glass onto the table between them, he took that as a sign that he had her full attention.

"Do you…?" He scrubbed at the back of his neck with his fingers, nerves rising. "Do you want to decorate the tree?"

As though snapping alert from some dream, Samantha's spine pulled taut and she clapped her hands to her thighs. "Yes! The tree. Let's do that."

Noah bounded to his feet, unsure of what had just happened. Whatever it was, he knew Samantha felt it too, because she kept her distance as he opened the box and began sorting through the contents. Her hands traced up and down her arms, fidgety and flighty, while she peered over his shoulder.

"Let's plug these into the wall first and see what we're working with." Noah uncoiled a long, tangled strand of clear Christmas lights, searching for the end knotted up in the bunch. "I'm not sure what goes on in that box during the off season, but I swear there are always at least a dozen lights missing from the strands."

"They look so beautiful on the tree, but they sure are a hassle, aren't they? I love the vintage ones that my grandmother used to have. You know the kind I'm talking about? Those big, colorful ones?"

"I definitely remember those. One year my dad dropped an entire box of them and they shattered into a million pieces. Fragile little buggers."

"I guess there's no such thing as perfect Christmas

tree lighting, is there? I mean, weren't Christmas trees originally lit with candles?"

"An option our insurance policy doesn't cover at the Cedar Crest Cabins, unfortunately," he joked. "Eureka!" Thrusting the electrical prong into the air, Noah bellowed enthusiastically. "And now for the moment of truth."

Samantha clasped her hands together and did a little dance that looked more like a wobble. "Will it be a Christmas miracle?"

Pushing the prongs into the socket on the wall behind the tree, Noah held his breath. Much to his relief, the entire strand lit up with hundreds of shining lights, every one sparkling brilliantly, like little stars in the sky. "Would you look at that?"

"I can honestly say I've never seen that happen. I'm usually the one rushing out to the store to buy more strands while Mom and Dad start with the garland. Those lights never seem to last more than one year. I'd say you got your money's worth out of this bunch."

"It's a good thing these are in working order because I don't want you going anywhere in this storm." He didn't want her going anywhere, period, but he didn't add that.

"It's supposed to be a big one?"

"Biggest of the season, so far. Funny, really, because none of that was in the forecast when we planned the shoot. I guess it's a good thing the commercial was canceled after all. There's no way we'd be able to film in the blizzard-like conditions they're predicting."

"Everything works out the way it should," Samantha said with a brief nod. She took hold of the other end of the light strand and tucked it into the dense evergreen branches. "I'm a firm believer in that."

"I am, too."

From the opposite side of the tree, Noah met her gaze and smiled. The glittering way the lights highlighted her features made her even more radiant than before, and Noah wasn't sure that was possible. He gently cleared his throat.

"Should we get these put on?" he asked, holding up his side of the bundle of lights and giving it a shake. Samantha nodded.

They rotated their way in reverse directions, twining the lights onto the tapered branches of the stately evergreen. After several spins, they met up in the middle, all but bumping into one another.

"Sorry!" Samantha blurted. "Got a little wound up there."

"Funny, since your original plan was to *un*wind tonight," Noah kidded. Samantha flashed an appreciative smile, noting his comedic attempt. She sure knew how to make him feel good, even if she was only humoring him.

Tucking the last portion of lights into the fir, Noah stepped back. Samantha did the same. There they stood before the newly illuminated Christmas tree, shoulder to shoulder, hands lined up, fingertips grazing. He vividly remembered the first time he'd held a girl's hand back in high school and the nerves he had then were nothing compared to the ones plaguing his muddled mind, racing heart, and quivering stomach now. He held his breath, clamped his eyes shut, and moved his hand a fraction closer.

CHAPTER 13

"Got any garland in that box?" The volume at which her words left her mouth made Samantha jolt even more than the feather-light feel of Noah's fingertip brushing hers. She hadn't intended to shout, but the tension was so thick that she couldn't come up with any other way to barrel through it.

Noah's gaze swung down to hers. He rapidly jammed his hands into his pockets and paused a moment before speaking, eyes roving over her face. "Garland? Uh…no…I didn't see any."

Emphatically lifting her hands in the air, Samantha declared, "We can't have a tree without garland! We must remedy this immediately!"

"I think there might be some popcorn we could pop back in the dining hall kitchen. I could grab some fishing line, too. Would that work?"

"That would be perfect." In two quick strides she

was at the coat rack to retrieve her jacket, thrusting her hands into the armholes, grip on the door handle. "Let's go!"

"You can't go outside like that."

"Like what?" She knew she wasn't at her most fashionable, but she sincerely doubted they would come into contact with anyone who might judge her appearance at this hour.

Noah nudged his chin as his eyes lifted to the top of her head. "With your hair wet. You'll freeze. Can't have that."

Warmth spread through her, endeared by his concern. "You're right. I didn't think about that. Do you mind waiting while I blow dry it? I won't be long."

"Take all the time you need."

As the dryer hummed in her ear, Samantha scolded herself. Why was she acting like such an excitable fool? Sure, she hadn't dated in longer than she dared to admit, but she wasn't a complete stranger to the world of flirting. But that's not exactly what they were doing here. She liked Noah, and every moment spent with him uncovered more reasons for that fondness to grow. He'd expressed concern about her going outside with wet hair, after all. They weren't just casually flirting; they were getting to know one another. But the intentions behind their interactions…Samantha couldn't be certain.

As promised, Samantha made quick work of drying her hair and five minutes later, she emerged from the bathroom, ready to join Noah on their garland hunt. His back was to her, hands shoved deep into his pant's pockets, head inclined toward the very tip of the tree.

"It's really beautiful with only the lights, isn't it?" Samantha crossed the room to meet him.

"I was just remembering when we used to decorate our tree as a family. Even when we were really little, Mom and Dad would always let us be a part of it—choosing which ornament would go where and if we wanted clear or colored lights. With three unruly boys, Mom would worry about letting us use the hooks, and for good reason. She ultimately made us hang everything with a loop of red string instead."

He pointed to a thin, pale line intersecting one eyebrow. Samantha hadn't noticed it before, the way it left a jagged ridge in the hairs arching over his right eye.

"David snagged me one year when he pretended to use it as a fishing hook. My mom got so mad, but Dad just said, 'I think you should throw that one back, Davie.' Dad got a lot of mileage out of that joke. His effortless humor is something I'll always remember about him." Noah's gaze traveled up and down the tree. "It's funny how when you're a kid, you don't realize you're always right in the middle of a memory."

Awareness rushed through Samantha, his words not lost on her. She knew full well the beautiful memory they were in the midst of creating, and she dreaded the thought of their interactions—her time spent at Cedar Crest Cabins—becoming her past instead of her present. She just wasn't ready for that.

"What do you say we track down some garland?" Propping out his elbow, Noah rotated toward her and Samantha slid her hand into the crook he created. He tugged her ever-so-slightly closer to his side as they ducked out the front door and into the frosty night air.

The sky was starless, the dense blanket of suspended clouds buffering the celestial tapestry above it. Even the moon was tucked away. Other than the muted porch light glow from the dining hall several yards ahead, their surroundings were shadowy and dim. Samantha relied on Noah to guide the way and kept her eyes trained on her feet as they navigated across the snowy terrain.

When they made it to the door, Noah paused.

"After you." Like a gentleman, he ushered her in first, then let the door fall softly into place at their backs. "The kitchen is straight through those swinging doors along the far wall."

The dining hall was vastly different at night, tables unset and chairs empty. Even the piano in the corner of the room was lifeless without the joyful swell of music ringing from its ivory keys. It dawned on Samantha that the true magic of Cedar Crest didn't dwell in the cabins or the structures or even the property, but within the people who inhabited it.

Before her contemplation fully took hold, a clatter interrupted her thoughts.

Noah froze. "Did you hear that?" he whispered in her ear. He urged her body even closer to his.

Another clang, followed by a metallic sounding crash, spurred Noah into immediate action. He rushed forward and flung the saloon-like doors apart. The wooden partitions rattled on their hinges as they forcefully crashed open against the walls.

An ear-splitting shriek made Samantha's blood run cold.

"Vera! What are you doing here?" Noah flipped the lights on a nearby switch.

Vera whirled around, eyes squinting against the intrusive glare. "What am *I* doing here? What are you doing barging in on a famished, pregnant woman like that? You could make your entry a little less startling, you know. That fright was enough to put me into labor!" Rallying her breath, Vera's chest heaved.

"I thought you were a raccoon."

"I could be likened to a lot of animals lately— hippo, elephant, even a moose—but a raccoon isn't one of them."

"All that rummaging around. I just assumed our resident raccoon was back, wreaking havoc again. I was prepared to discover a complete mess when I came through those doors."

From behind her back, Vera brandished a carton of mint chocolate chip ice cream, a guilty expression sweeping over her features. "Nope. Just me rummaging around for some late night, sugary sustenance. Care to join me? I can grab a couple extra spoons."

"We're actually here to find some popcorn," Noah declined. "We're currently on a garland making mission for Samantha's tree."

"I know we have some of that around here. That was last week's craving. Top shelf on the left." Indicating the direction with the tip of her spoon, Vera nodded toward the cupboard above the commercial grade refrigerator. "I'll get the stove ready."

Within minutes, their garland preparation was well underway. The consistent pop, pop, pop of kernels ricocheting against the shallow saucepan created an energetic buzz that brought Samantha's senses to life, despite the late hour. Their laughter, Noah and Vera's sibling-in-law banter, and the crackling of popped corn all combined as the soundtrack Samantha would forever tie to this very moment once it became a memory.

They were four batches deep when David discovered them. He walked into the kitchen with much less fanfare than his brother had, and his slippered feet and robe tied around his middle suggested he'd been set to retire already.

"I figured I'd find you here." He came up to his wife and deposited a loving kiss on the crown of her hair. "Didn't think I'd find you, though," he directed toward Noah and yawned. "You planning some epic movie night I didn't get the invite to?" David dipped his hand into one of the large serving bowls and scooped out a fistful of popcorn, lifting it to his mouth.

Noah swatted him, sending the popped kernels into the air like a dozen launched snowballs. "This popcorn is not meant for consumption," Noah corrected. "It's garland for Samantha's tree."

David gave his brother a look Samantha spotted, though she figured she wasn't meant to. She caught the tiny smile on Vera's lips, too.

"I think that's plenty, don't you?" Samantha shook the last batch from the pan into a fresh bowl.

"Yep. Should be enough," Noah agreed.

"Then let's get started." She looked around the kitchen, noticing the lack of chairs or tables to work at. "Should we set up out in the dining hall?"

"I don't know about you, but I can't sit in those wooden chairs for more than a few minutes without my sciatic nerve acting up." Hand pressed low on her back, Vera suggested, "Why don't we head up to Noah's apartment? I claim the recliner!"

She wasn't sure why, but Samantha had never given much thought to Noah's living situation. She knew he likely resided on the property somewhere, but that was as far as that thought played out.

"Sure. We can go up there." Noah lifted a bowl from the counter. "Everyone grab a bowl."

David opened a door at the back of the kitchen and led the way with Noah bringing up the rear. A narrow wooden staircase spiraled up to a studio apartment. The iron railing was glazed with a fresh scattering of snow and, without anything to grip onto, Samantha felt shakily off balance. The hand that came to rest gently on the small of her back surprised her at first, but gratefulness surpassed any feelings of unease. The last thing she wanted to do was fall.

"Careful," Noah spoke softly, "it can get a little slippery."

His home was modest and less cabin-like in feel than the other structures on the property. There were a few family photographs on the mantle and a large, fresh wreath with a velvety bow was strung up over the fireplace. The chair Vera mentioned was well worn and had a bulky blanket draped over the back, ready to be snuggled within its hand-knit warmth. Immediately, Vera waddled her way toward the chair and plopped down. The aged leather hissed beneath her.

"Alright, now hand me my bowl!" She flapped her hands toward David, who walked over and settled one of the popcorn containers onto the side table next to her.

"Let me grab that fishing line." Noah crossed the room and hunkered down low to access a cabinet beneath the sink. From where she stood, Samantha could see an aged, rusted toolbox next to an equally used tackle box, the kind that was likely passed down from generation to generation. She assumed it had belonged to Noah's father—maybe even his grandfather—and her heart ached at the lack of heirlooms within her own family.

She didn't want them to be hoarders necessarily, but she wished her parents weren't so purge-happy, always tossing things out that they deemed unessential. She would love to have something from her father's childhood, but she supposed having him around was the true blessing.

"Found it!"

After passing around the items needed to construct their garland strands, Noah came to sit next to Samantha on a corduroy couch, a bowl of popcorn wedged between them. David had been fiddling with a stereo in the media cabinet, and once he found the station he searched for, he rested on the generous arm of the recliner, angling his body close to his wife's as she strung the popcorn puffs onto the clear line.

The dulcet crooning of Bing Crosby's *I'll Be Home for Christmas* emanated from the speakers, melodic and full. That particular song made Samantha's heart catch and while she loved it so, she knew it had been originally written during wartime, the lyrics from the perspective of a young soldier longing for home. It was the final line that consistently made Samantha's throat scratch with unspent tears. She couldn't imagine being home for Christmas only in a dream. She tried to maintain her composure as the heart-tugging song carried on, but the mist that gleamed in her eyes couldn't be blinked away.

"Hey. You okay?" Noah rotated to look at her, his presence feeling even closer.

"I'm fine," she answered with a sniff. "That song just always gets to me."

"Me too," Vera agreed from her comfy chair. Tears streamed down her cheeks and while Samantha felt for her obvious display of emotion, she was comforted by the fact that she wasn't alone. "These dang hormones!" Vera shoved a hand against her jawline to sop up the tears. "Would you believe I cried at a dog food commercial the other day? I'm a mess!"

"I don't think you have to be hormonal to agree that everyone should be home—or have a home—for the holidays," Noah assured, and when Samantha dipped her hand back into the popcorn bowl to retrieve another popped kernel for her strand, Noah caught it. He looked her in the eyes and gave it a squeeze. "What if we did that?"

"Did what?" David glanced up from his work. Of the four, his strand was the longest, coiling like a snake in a twisted pile on the floor.

"Provided a home for the holiday."

"That was the original plan, brother. To make a commercial that would generate some Christmas bookings."

"I know that, but I'm not talking about paid reservations."

David paused and lowered his needle and fishing line to his lap, head cocked. "I don't follow."

"What if we used our cabins a little differently? You always hear stories of families needing places to gather for the holidays, right? Well, we have a place—

a dozen of them, in fact—and I think we should donate them for that cause."

Samantha's heart picked up speed as Noah expounded on his thoughts. She loved where he was going with this.

"When my brother was at the children's hospital —before he passed—patients would come from all over the country for medical treatments. More often than not, their families would have to stay in a nearby hotel, sometimes for months at a time. Are you thinking of using your cabins for something like that?"

"That's exactly what I'm thinking. Anyone who wouldn't normally be able to afford a Christmas at the cabins. They'll be welcome here."

"Noah, *we* can hardly afford a Christmas at the cabins. Our debt is growing and while I appreciate where your heart is on this, I just don't see how it's possible." David skewered a piece of popcorn with his needle, his mouth contorting into a sympathetic frown. "Financially speaking, we would need a miracle."

Noah's hand released Samantha's. He got back to work on his strand. "Well then, we're in luck because I do believe that's exactly what this time of year is all about."

CHAPTER 14

*N*oah's new hope for the cabins kept him up most of the night, along with the wind that tore through the summit, whipping and whirling with gusts forceful enough to uproot a grandiose fir tree. He wasn't sure which distraction rattled his brain more—the budding idea or the growing storm—and come morning, the dark circles slung under his eyes and overall groggy countenance bore witness to his fitful attempt at slumber.

"You look like you got into a fight with a grizzly and the grizzly won each and every round," Grandma Kitty mused as she poured Noah a much needed cup of coffee. "This should perk you right up."

The zesty blend of cinnamon and dark roast beans woke him up a touch, but he'd require several mugs full before anyone could label him perky.

"Thanks, Grandma. Didn't sleep well."

Kitty's wrinkled hand came down on top of his.

"Listen, Noah. This whole commercial thing isn't your fault. I know you often bear the burden of responsibility around here, but we're all in this together." She scooted out a dining chair and sat at the table, placing the pot of coffee in front of her. "We will come up with something. If we put all of our heads together, I know we can."

"I think I might already have an idea. It's actually what kept me up all night."

He wanted to elaborate, but their few remaining guests started to trickle into the dining room—couple by couple—and he knew his grandmother would want to ensure they received a proper greeting and warm breakfast. After all, this was her favorite part of running the lodge.

"Go." He encouraged her with a smile. "I can fill you in later. There's still a lot I need to work out."

"I can't wait to hear all about it, sweetie." Pressing up onto wobbly legs, Kitty took the handle of the pot back into her grip and shuffled her way over to the breakfast buffet, calling out morning pleasantries and salutations with genuine affection.

His grandmother was such a wonderful host, hospitable and social in a way the rest of them could only strive to emulate. His mother, Audrey, was equally gracious, but he knew she preferred the tasks that allowed her to stay behind the scenes. The only exception was when she took her place at the piano. It was there that she blossomed, opening up with each note and song.

They all had their talents, not unlike the clients at Samantha's agency. The thing was, none of them had auditioned for this gig, and in truth, Noah wasn't sure how they were going to pull it all off.

His brother wasn't wrong when he'd said it might take a miracle.

Noah sat and savored his morning coffee, feeling a little remorseful that David was already canvassing the snow-covered mountainside on the plow. But he knew his brother loved running that big, old machine, so Noah didn't let that guilt settle. They all had their roles to play and specific shoes to fill.

Noah didn't realize he'd been intentionally waiting for her, but when the last guest finished their morning meal and Samantha still hadn't shown, the sinking sensation that hollowed out his stomach took him by surprise. It shocked him that in just a couple of short days, he'd grown so used to her company. Used to seeing her around the cabins. Used to her sweet laugh and lovely voice he could already pick out in any crowd. He looked forward to their encounters, and he only hoped she felt the same.

While he'd wanted to share breakfast, he suddenly had an even better idea.

"I'm so glad you asked me to lunch." Samantha directed her gaze across the cab of Noah's Jeep. Her eyes twinkled as they locked in on his, and her smile matched the one he'd been wearing from the moment she climbed into his vehicle. "I did not intend to sleep through breakfast. Something about the storm last night—that constant hum of the wind against the cabin—lulled me to sleep like a baby."

Even though it had had the opposite effect on him, he was grateful Samantha was well rested. She certainly looked it with her bright green eyes and giddy demeanor that was almost catching. She practically bounced in her seat with enthusiasm for the day.

"Oh goodness, my stomach is sure angry at me!" She smothered her waist with her palm, right above her lap belt. "Did you hear that enormous growl?"

"I didn't, but I'm glad to hear you're hungry. The place I'm taking you serves portions big enough to feed Santa, all his reindeer, and his entire team of elves."

"Let me guess." She thumbed her chin, eyes dancing with mischief. "It's an old movie theatre and they serve food in popcorn buckets. No, wait—it's a retrofitted high school and you eat in the cafeteria."

"Nope and nope. But close." He flipped on his blinker and maneuvered the Jeep into the next lane. "It's an old barn and they built each booth into a horse stall, with long, rustic dining tables spaced out in the center aisle. Thankfully, they don't make you eat out of a trough and there's more on the menu than just apples and carrots."

"The creativity in these parts amazes me."

"I think it's more resourcefulness than it is creativity. It's expensive to build up here, and not all that easy to get materials delivered. And that's if you can convince a construction crew it's worth their time to even take on work in this area. It honestly makes more sense to use something existing and modify it to meet your needs."

Which was exactly what he wanted to do with the cabins. Part of his plan in inviting Samantha to lunch was to pick her brain regarding the issue. Of the four, she seemed to be the most on board last night. Not that David was discouraging or that he flat-out disagreed, he just tempered Noah's excitement with undeniable reality.

But sometimes it was necessary to dream big, think outside the box, and trust the impossible could happen. Noah believed that in his core.

As he had hoped she would, Samantha found *The Big White Barn* to be every bit as endearing as *The Guzzler.* She appreciated the ingenuity and while Noah couldn't take credit, there was a bit of small town pride that puffed up with each approving comment.

"I can't believe we're eating in a horse stall," she said after they'd been seated. She peered over her menu toward Noah on the other side of the booth. "This is so fun."

"Just be thankful they mucked it out first."

That got him a laugh and the smile he had come to crave from Samantha. "So, what are you getting? I'm leaning toward the Buckaroo BLT. But the Lasso Lamb Chop looks good, too. I can't decide."

"I'm a sucker for the Chuck Wagon Cheeseburger. Get it every time."

When the server came to their stall, they ordered, even though Samantha vacillated between three different options before finalizing her decision in a flustered rush.

"I'm usually not so indecisive," she said, almost shameful.

"There are loads of good choices on that menu. You're not being indecisive, just exploring your options. No harm in that."

"That's a very kind way of putting it. Oliver certainly never saw it that way." She looked down at her lap, hands fiddling with the checkered cloth napkin draped across it. "He'd get so frustrated with me when we would try to agree on a place to eat or a movie to see. He'd outright turn the car around and head home if we couldn't come to a decision in a designated amount of time. I felt like a child who had done something wrong."

A defensive rush swept through Noah, like his hackles were suddenly raised. "I'm sorry you had to go through that, Samantha. But I'm glad you got out of it."

She nodded. "In the end, the split was mutual. I'm sure there were just as many things he couldn't tolerate about me as there were grievances I had toward him."

"I find that very hard to believe."

"You flatter me, Noah. But I've got faults. More than a few of them."

He had yet to discover any, but he knew no one was perfect. What he wouldn't give for the gift of more time with this woman. The time to discover her nuances and quirks. Likes and dislikes. And yes, even her faults, though he figured they were limited.

"I know you didn't bring me here to listen to me prattle on about my ex-husband and our marital strife. Was there something you wanted to talk to me about?"

Noah adjusted his position on the pine bench, the boards creaking beneath his weight. "Do you think my idea to donate the cabins for the season is crazy?"

She brought her water cup to her mouth and held it there while she thought on his words, eyes connecting with his over the rim. "Do I think it's crazy? Not at all. In my book, generosity is never crazy." Taking a sip, she swallowed and then drew in a deep breath before lowering her glass to the table. "But I do share your brother's worry that it might financially bankrupt you. The entire goal with the commercial was to market your cabins and drum up some business. I worry if you don't start with anything in the bank, you'll never climb your way out of debt."

He subscribed to that belief, too, and that was the most dejecting part of it all. There was no money to make any of this happen. There weren't even funds to hire a camera crew to film a commercial anymore, for

Pete's sake. What made him think he could magically turn nothing into something?

"You're right." He raked a hand through his hair. "It feels like we've been pushing a boulder uphill all this time. But this idea to use the property for something other than profit—it's the first time I've been excited to carry on the Cedar Crest Cabins legacy in longer than I can remember."

Samantha nodded slowly, hanging on his words with sincere, rapt interest. Even when their food arrived at the table and they started in on their lunch, she kept engaged by asking questions and offering her ideas, and together they chatted about the history of Cedar Crest throughout the duration of their meal. Noah's new hope for the cabins' purpose took deeper root within him as they talked, and even though he knew it was unlikely he could pull it off, he wasn't willing to discard his dream just yet.

At the end of their meal, just as he was signing the check that Samantha had offered to split but he refused, her phone trilled from within her purse.

"I'm sorry." She dipped her hand into her bag. "I meant to turn my ringer off."

"Take it. I don't mind."

Samantha's mouth flipped and her eyebrows buckled when she read the Caller ID. "It's Oliver. I should probably get this. It might be about work."

"Not a problem." Noah slid his credit card into his wallet and then returned the leather billfold to his back pocket. He tried not to eavesdrop on the conversation, but their proximity made it difficult not to.

"Not that I can recall," Samantha spoke into the mouthpiece. "I believe Netty Williams had her baby last summer. She was the only maternity model I represented. When would you need someone?"

Noah gathered it was about work, just as Samantha had suspected. From what he could decipher from the one-sided conversation, it sounded as though Oliver needed a pregnant model, and quickly. Coincidentally enough, Noah happened to know one very pregnant, very local option.

"Vera?" he mouthed.

Samantha's eyes locked on his. "Wait a second, Oliver. I just might be able to help you out with a maternity model after all. But there's one important question—how flexible is the production crew?"

CHAPTER 15

"I told Oliver they would have to film it here," Samantha said as she withdrew an ornament from the cardboard box and threaded a hook through the small eye. "And they only get one full day of shooting with the crew. We get the second."

Noah lifted a glittering red bauble from the shredded newspaper and hung it on the uppermost branch. "Do you think we'll be ready to shoot a commercial? We don't even have a workable script."

"We'll have to be."

She didn't like these types of negotiations, but it was their only feasible option. And it was mutually beneficial: Oliver got his maternity model and the Jensens would get another shot at filming a commercial for their cabins. It was a win-win on paper, but she could still sense Noah's lingering disappointment.

"Maybe this year you should just try to ramp up

bookings the traditional way, through marketing and advertising," she had suggested at the end of their lunch earlier that day. "Put some cash in the bank. Then you can roll out your *Home for the Holidays* idea next Christmas, once the cabins are profitable again."

Her words were met with a surrendered shrug and equally defeated nod. "I think you're probably right," he'd conceded, though she knew it pained him to do so. "Seems like it's our only choice."

They hadn't talked more about it until now, and Samantha knew her timing was terribly off. Who wanted to dwell on dashed hopes while decorating a holiday tree?

"Listen, we can work out all the commercial details tomorrow. I know a really great script writer I can reach out to. I've worked with him in the past on a few projects. Who knows, maybe he'll have some ideas for us," she assured, but it felt like a useless Hail Mary. "It will all work out in the end."

"I know it will." The warm smile Noah directed at her instantly set Samantha at ease. He certainly had a way of doing that.

For the next hour, they trimmed the tree, outfitting it fully with red, white, and silver ball ornaments placed within the winding strands of fluffy popcorn and lustrous twinkle lights. Just as Noah stretched to position the star at the top of the tree, a soft rap on the door halted his action. He froze as though caught in the middle of a game of tag.

"Kitty!" Samantha greeted ecstatically, surprised

when she saw the Jensen matriarch on the other side of the threshold. "Come on in. We're just finishing up decorating my tree. You must see it. It's turning out to be quite a stunner."

"Did I get here in time for the topper?" Grandma Kitty slipped out of her jacket while stepping into the cabin. "You know that's my favorite part."

"I do remember that." Noah held out the star. "Would you like to do the honors, Grandma? I'd be happy to give you a boost."

"Noah, dear, I'd have to climb onto your shoulders to reach the top of that magnificent tree." She waved him off and hung her jacket on the coat rack. "I'll leave it to you, sweetheart. Don't need any trips to the emergency room tonight."

Kitty came to stand next to Samantha. "Brought you a little something." She passed off a small package wrapped in brown craft paper that had been concealed under her arm.

"You brought *me* something? You didn't need to do that." Slipping her finger under a piece of tape, Samantha popped free the folded paper. When she saw Noah had clearly been waiting on the two women, she hugged the package to her chest. "I'm so sorry, Noah! Go ahead with the topper. First things first."

"I'm happy to wait." He grinned and settled the star onto the coffee table before taking a seat on the couch. "If it's what I think it is, you'll want to open that right away."

Samantha couldn't possibly imagine what this unexpected gift might be. Hurriedly tearing through the wrapping paper, she let the parchment flutter to the floor.

"Oh, Kitty." Her breath hitched. "It's beautiful!"

"Your name is a long one, but thankfully, it all fits."

Samantha stared down at the personalized stocking in her hands, fibers of bright green and deep crimson spelling out her name across the top. At the base, near the 'foot', was a felt Santa appliqué, sewn directly onto the handmade holiday creation.

"You knitted this?"

"Sure did. This cabin is the only one that didn't already have stockings decorating the mantle. I figured if I was going to make one, I might as well personalize it." Kitty curled a hand around Samantha's shoulder and squeezed. "Something to remember us by, sweetheart."

Samantha didn't need a physical memento to remember the Jensens. They had already etched a permanent mark on her heart.

"This is so thoughtful, Kitty. I love it. Thank you."

"You're welcome. Now, should we let Noah finally put that star on the top of this fine-looking tree? What do you say, grandson? You ready?"

"Let's do it."

It certainly wasn't the tree-lighting at Rockefeller Center, but when Noah nestled the rustic, wooden star onto the highest point of the Christmas tree,

Samantha knew she was standing before something just as special. Maybe even more so.

She warmed with absolute gladness.

"It's perfect," she whispered.

"It is," Noah echoed, his eyes trained solely on her.

Snapping to attention, Kitty clapped her hands together. "Alright, kiddos. It's past my bedtime. This old gal needs her beauty sleep and lots of it. Off I go."

"I'll walk you back to your cabin," Noah started, but Kitty cut him off.

"Nope." She patted his forearm and winked. "You stay right here. Believe it or not, I do know my way around this place."

Even though she refused his chivalry, Noah waited at the open door until his grandmother was out of sight, the steadily falling snow blurring her outline with each step. Only when she was no longer visible did he close the door and return to the couch where Samantha waited, turning over the stocking in her hands. She admired every inch of it and knew this was a treasure she would hold dear for many Christmases to come.

"If you can't tell, gift giving is my grandma's love language," Noah said.

"It's such a thoughtful gift. I almost feel bad that my name is so long." Samantha traced a finger over the knit letters, spelling them out with the tip of her index finger.

"You can't help having a long name."

"Well." She made a face. "I actually have a pretty short one. Samantha's technically my middle name."

Noah's mouth curled. "Is that right?"

"Yep. And once you hear my legal name, you'll know exactly why I go by Samantha instead."

"I see. Why do I have the feeling this is something I have to guess?" he asked, interest obviously piqued.

"What would be the fun in outright telling you?"

"Okay, okay. I'm up for a little guessing game. Can you at least give me a hint? What does it start with?"

Samantha pursed her lips and shook her head tightly. "Nope. No clues. You're all on your own with this."

"No clues?"

"Not a one."

"How am I supposed to narrow down from—I don't know—a few million options?"

Samantha thought on it, realizing it wasn't entirely fair to leave Noah altogether clueless. There certainly was a seemingly endless array of women's names to select from. Maybe *one* little clue wouldn't hurt.

"One clue." She held up a finger to count it off. "But only one. You ready?"

"I'm ready."

"It's also the name of a plant."

She could see the hint tumbling around in his brain as his eyes squinted under a pensive, focused brow. "Fern?" he posited, though he lacked any sort of confidence in his guess.

"No." Samantha tried not to grimace. "And thank goodness for that."

He took a few more moments before attempting a second guess, then speculated cautiously, "Daisy?"

"Daisy Day? That's really cute, but no again."

"And you're not going to give me another clue? Can we narrow this down? Is it a flower? A tree? A shrub?"

"You're not getting anything else out of me." With her thumb and finger, she pretended to lock an imaginary key at her lips. "I already gave you a very generous clue, if I do say so myself."

"It was a good one. I agree. But I'm scrolling through a long list in my head and none seem to fit. Rose. Sage. Lily."

"All good names, none of which are on my birth certificate."

He tossed out more guesses at random, and Samantha knew the exact moment it came to him. She could almost see the light bulb flash behind his eyes when Noah locked in on the answer. His shoulders pulled taut, face full of disbelief.

"They wouldn't," he said in skeptical, slow words.

"Oh, they did," Samantha confirmed. "I mean, have you *met* my parents?"

"They really named you Holly?"

"Sure did. Holly Day. I mean, were they trying to punish me?"

"I think it's adorable."

Samantha rolled her eyes. "I lasted one Christmas season in elementary school before I figured out I was in for a lifetime of ridicule if I didn't do something. I even changed schools just so I could start completely over. New school. New name. New me."

"So you've been going by Samantha the majority of your life, then?"

"I have. Only a handful of people even know my real name is Holly. It's not something I share very often."

"I consider it an honor to be added to that list." Noah stretched his arm along the back of the couch. It felt as close to having his arm draped over her shoulder as she could imagine, and the thought sent a welcome tingle skittering up her spine. "Thank you for sharing that piece of yourself with me."

"I figure, at the very least, it's good for a laugh."

"I'm not laughing." Noah's voice came out in a muted, vulnerable tone. "I love that your parents are so passionate about all things Christmas. That's something they share with my family."

"But yours haven't taken it to the extreme like mine have. They must have known what they were doing when they named me that. They had to."

"Have you ever asked them?"

"I have. Dad said it was the perfect name for a baby girl born on Christmas. That he couldn't *not* name me Holly."

"Wait! Your birthday is on Christmas Day?"

"It is," Samantha confirmed in what sounded more like a groan than an audible answer. "Again, not something I tell everybody."

"Samantha, this is—"

"Mind boggling?"

"No. It's great! I mean, of course I can see how you might not love it, especially growing up. But I happen to think it's appropriately quirky and downright endearing."

She offered a weak smile. "I've learned to have a good attitude about it, I suppose. When I was a kid, I always hated having my birthday on Christmas because it inevitably meant fewer presents. But as I got older, I realized the physical presents weren't what it was all about, anyway. Things like family. Faith. Those are the true gifts of the season. The things you can't unwrap. So I guess I don't mind that my birthday is on Christmas anymore." Samantha shrugged her shoulders to her ears and let them drop. "But I'm still a little peeved they went so far as to name me Holly. That's just cruel."

"You know, we could really work with this. The whole *Home for the Holly-days* thing." He nudged her gently right between her ribs, smirking with mirth. "I can see it now. 'Come stay at the cabins that are Holly Day approved!' You could totally be the face of the Cedar Crest Cabins."

"Very funny." She rolled her eyes again with great exaggeration. "The Jensens will always be the face of these cabins."

"My hope is that it's less about the Jensens and more about the Christmas spirit around here. That's what I want for this place. I just want us all to be in the background."

"I know you do, Noah. Your humility is what I love most about you."

It was just an innocent word wedged into the middle of her sentence, but it felt like a deep confession as it left her lips. She wouldn't deny its truth, though. She did love that about Noah—his genuine modesty and humble nature. She actually loved lots of little things about him. Each loveable characteristic stacked on top of the other, making her heart squeeze each time she thought of him. One day, she imagined all of that admiration could build into something that felt a lot like being in love romantically, but she knew it was too soon to tell.

"I appreciate that, Samantha. And I appreciate you. That you're still here. That you've given us a lot of grace even though we've messed everything up."

Her hand came down and touched his. "Let me ask you something. Right here, right now, does it feel like you've messed anything up?"

CHAPTER 16

The expectant look on Samantha's face translated clearly. Her eyes meandered idly over Noah's face, tracking across his skin until they fastened onto his mouth, pausing there. Absolute awareness heightened the moment, and it was as though his senses were on overdrive, everything magnified.

The fire crackled louder within the hearth. The Christmas tree stood taller, its thick, pine scent more potent than he previously remembered it. Even the tempo of his heart and the shallowness of his breath that escaped him left him dizzied and swirling like he'd been caught up in a shaken snow globe.

Shifting on the loveseat, he pressed closer, head inclining nearer to Samantha's.

"Is it…?" Noah cleared his throat softly. "Is it alright if I kiss you?"

Ruby lips that had been slightly parted widened

into a full-fledged grin. "Thought you would never ask."

That was all the invitation—and shot of confidence—Noah needed. His hand found the back of Samantha's neck and his fingers curled to urge her closer. It wasn't a large sofa to begin with, but it suddenly became smaller, their bodies drawn together as his lips came down over hers. The breathy sigh Samantha released served as an agreement. Every question he'd had about his rising feelings being purely one-sided vanished like a swirling snowflake in the artic wind.

His last kiss had been several years back. That uneventful kiss broke his dry spell, but nothing more than that. This kiss with Samantha—it broke so many of Noah's promises, namely the one that vowed to focus only on the success of the cabins. He didn't have time for a budding relationship, if that's what this could even turn into. But he shoved those pestering thoughts into the recesses of his mind for now. The only thing that deserved his attention was the incredible woman in his arms.

Kissing Samantha was all things good. Thrilling like the pulsing rush of adrenaline from a downhill sled race. Sweet and spicy, like the tangy bite of a gingerbread cookie. Warm and satisfying like a long-dreamt for wish finally fulfilled. It was as though they already knew this intimate part of one another, and at the same time, it was new and fresh and exciting in ways Noah had never experienced.

There was a shared tenderness that made Noah's heart ache not with pain, but with gratitude that someone like Samantha had shown up in his life unannounced. Wound her way into his heart. Eased her way into his hopes.

They kissed for what felt like hours, though time seemed to both stand still and race by all at once. He would've kissed her until daybreak and been content in doing so had the startling knock on the door not drawn them out of their kiss and from one another's arms.

"You expecting anyone?" Noah rallied his breath.

Samantha ran her thumb along her bottom lip. "I'm not. Are you?"

Head shaking, Noah stood from the sofa just as another succession of knocks rattled the door.

"Coming!"

Occasionally, a wayward traveler would stop by after hours to inquire about potential vacancies, but they usually came straight to the lodge and didn't knock on cabin doors at random. This knowledge caused Noah to puff up a little taller, just in case this unanticipated visitor posed some sort of threat. He doubted that to be the situation, but one could never be too cautious.

The person on the other side of the door was halfway into another round of knocking when Noah finally pulled down on the handle.

A man dressed in clothes too fine and expensive for the rugged outdoors stood opposite him. If Noah had to guess, he was right around his age, though there was an air of sophistication Noah would never match, no matter how up in years he got.

"Evening," Noah greeted. "Can I help you?"

"Evening," the man parroted as he smoothed the front of his jacket with the palm of his leather driving gloves. "I'm looking for Samantha Day. I was told I would be able to find her in this cabin."

Noah's stomach churned, suspicion heightened. "Who is asking?"

"Her husband."

He hadn't noticed her movement behind him, but Noah suddenly felt Samantha's presence at his back, and when her fingers wound with his own in a possessive hold, that high-alert wariness dropped.

"*Ex*-husband," she corrected. "Oliver, what on earth are you doing here?"

"I've been keeping tabs on the weather app and thought I'd seize the opportunity to head up the hill in between storms. It's supposed to pick back up tomorrow. You and I both know the Maserati wouldn't do well in a blizzard." Oliver's eyes traveled down to where Noah and Samantha's hands joined.

"It's hardly going to be a blizzard," Samantha said in a tone Noah barely recognized from her. He wasn't sure she was even aware of it, but her fingers had a near death-grip on his. He ran his thumb over the back of her hand, hoping to ease her anxiety however he could.

"Either way, I thought it best to come sooner

rather than later." Oliver swung his rolling suitcase into the room first, right between Noah and Samantha, forcing them to release their grasp. They stepped back as Oliver then shoved his way into the middle of them, too. "I'm exhausted, Sam. You mind if I snag that quilt from the bed? Maybe a pillow, too? That's all I should need to make up the couch for tonight."

"You're staying here?"

"It's the only option. The girl at the desk said the only available rooms still needed to be cleaned. I can move over to one of those tomorrow, but for tonight, it'll be like old times. Complete with me sleeping on the couch and everything."

If Noah were more like his brother, Marty, those words would've been enough to make his hands ball into fists. Something about the way Oliver backhandedly demeaned Samantha with his precisely chosen words and haughty nature made Noah itch with the desire to grab the man by his expensive lapel and shake him silly. The sensation was so foreign Noah almost couldn't interpret it for what it was: pure jealousy.

"I can get one of the extra rooms cleaned for you right now," Noah offered. His teeth clenched down hard. "Won't be a problem."

"Oh, that isn't necessary. But thank you. Samantha and I will be just fine, won't we?" Oliver ran a hand down Samantha's back in a familiar way. "Maybe you could get us another log for the fire, though. It's quite chilly in here. But only if it's not too much trouble."

The ball of muscle at the back of Noah's jaw ticked. "Of course. Not a problem."

Samantha's eyes pleaded with Noah, but he didn't know how to answer them.

"I'll go with you," she stated.

Any other time, he would've asked her to stay inside while he headed out into the snow. But the opportunity to talk with her out of Oliver's earshot was welcome. He took her coat from the stand and held it out for her arms to slide into. Then he jammed his on and fit his beanie onto his head with needless angst before opening the cabin door.

The cords of firewood were stored along the outside wall of the dining hall, and Noah made the quick walk without opening his mouth to speak. He had no clue what to say. He did, however, keep his hand secured tightly around Samantha's and that seemed appreciated, maybe even expected. When he got to work sorting through the logs, Samantha finally broke their stilted silence.

"I didn't realize he would be coming tonight, Noah. I would have told you, had I known."

He chucked a few smaller pieces of wood to the side and withdrew the more sizeable logs. "I know you didn't."

"That's not exactly how I wanted to introduce you two, either. I had something different planned."

Hearing that she thought about how she would

introduce Noah to her friends and family caused Noah's heart to constrict. When was the last time a woman had wanted to show him off in that way?

"Oliver is a challenging man, but he's harmless."

"You feel comfortable with him staying in your cabin?"

"I do," she assured. "It's not my first choice, obviously, but it won't be an issue for one night. Knowing him, he's already sound asleep on the loveseat. Other than a little annoying snoring, he won't bother me at all."

Noah held an armful of split logs against his chest and breathed hotly through his mouth, the hazy, frozen air suspending between them. He looked down at Samantha, pained by the apologetic expression overlaying her features. Bending down, he placed the firewood into a small pile at his feet and then pressed back up to take her gently by the shoulders.

"I think I just wasn't prepared for the sudden interruption. I might've projected some of that frustration onto Oliver. Probably not entirely fair to do that."

"No, he's beyond frustrating. There's no arguing that. I'm honestly not really surprised he showed up unannounced. He's always had his own perturbing way of doing things." She huffed in annoyance and then gazed up at Noah with a sudden wash of sheer, unabashed eagerness. Standing all the way up onto her toes, Samantha's warm lips pushed to Noah's jaw.

"I didn't want the interruption, either," she said tenderly against his skin.

Turning his head, Noah caught Samantha's lips in a kiss that could've melted all the snow on the Cedar Crest mountainside. Their chemistry was off the charts, their fervor equally matched. Kissing Samantha was something he would never tire of; holding her was something he would desire every day of his life now that he knew just how good she felt encircled in his arms.

"I'm falling for you, Samantha." He pulled her close, his chin pressing into the crown of her thick hair. He breathed in deeply and said with a sigh, "I hope that's okay, because I honestly don't know how not to."

CHAPTER 17

*S*amantha sandwiched her cell phone between her ear and shoulder so her hands were free to apply another coat of mascara across her recently curled lashes. She rarely wore much makeup, but today she took a little longer with her morning routine. She was well aware some of that longing to look her very best had to do with Noah and their shared kiss the night before. Shared *kisses*, actually. Her entire body flushed red hot when she thought back on the recent memory.

For as much as she'd love to dive deep into her daydream, she reluctantly forced herself into the here and now.

"I don't even know what angle to come at this from anymore, Trish." Samantha ran the mascara wand over her lower lash line and took in her reflection in the oval bathroom mirror. "Anything will be better than the script they originally had, but gosh...I just feel like this place deserves something amazing. Something that is really going to sell it."

"I thought Santa was going to sell it," Trish replied. "Wasn't that the whole reason your parents were there auditioning?"

"Santa *was* going to sell it, and likely still is, but we don't have a script and the only reason we have a camera crew is because Oliver and I worked out a trade," she explained. "But there's no catchy jingle, let alone anyone to sing it. I feel more unprepared for this than I did for my driver's test and I failed that the first two times I took it!"

Trish's measured sigh came through the earpiece loud and clear, and Samantha took the hint that she was to follow suit. "Breathe, girl. Just breathe. As far as I can tell, none of this is your responsibility, right?"

"Technically, it's not. But I feel…I don't know… not an obligation, but this deep desire to get this place back on track."

"Does this deep desire have anything to do with Noah Jensen?"

The mascara wand slipped from Samantha's hands, ricocheting off the bathroom sink as it clattered around the porcelain basin, leaving smudges of black in its wake. "What? No!"

"Hey, I'm not judging. I did a little snooping. He's drop-dead gorgeous. Like rugged mountain man meets approachable guy next door."

"You did a little snooping? What does that mean?"

"I looked up their website. There's a big family photo of the Jensen clan on the *'About Us'* page," Trish admitted. "It took some sleuthing skills, but I'm pretty confident I narrowed it down to the right guy. I figured he wasn't the one with a wife and the other brother so isn't your type."

"I don't have a type."

"Yes, you do," Trish countered. "Noah gives off some serious Oliver vibes, I'd just like to point out."

Samantha choked on a gasp. "Well, that couldn't be further from the truth!"

"He's tall. Dark hair. Blue eyes. Girl, you definitely have a type. Noah checks all the boxes."

"Maybe he resembles Oliver looks-wise, but that's where the similarities begin and end."

"I'm glad to hear that. You know how I feel about Oliver."

Samantha did know. Oliver's partnership at the agency had been a huge road block for Trish back when Samantha was trying to get her to sign with Knight and Day.

"Assertive, off-putting, and too good-looking to be an honest man." Those were the words she had used for him, hitting the nail on the head with all three descriptors. Samantha had assured Trish that she wouldn't really have the need to work directly with Oliver and so far she'd been able to keep that promise. It was the main reason she was so hesitant to take this time off. She wouldn't dish her dear friend off on her ex, not if she could help it.

"What can I do?" Trish asked.

"You don't need to help with this, Trish. You've got a lot of exciting projects in the pipeline. Focus on those. I'll get all of this figured out," Samantha said. "Eventually."

"Yes, I do have projects in the pipeline, but those are in large part due to your hard work as my agent, I'd like to add. I'd be happy to help you however I can. You said you need someone to sing a jingle?"

"I mean, yeah, if we ever get one written."

"Then I'm your gal."

"Trish, I can't ask you to do that—"

"You better not tell me no because that will give me a serious complex," Trish said firmly. "If my own talent agent won't hire me for her personal project, then I must really be terrible!"

This was too much to request of someone. It was one thing for Samantha to throw herself into this endeavor. It was another thing altogether to rope her friend in.

"There's no budget, Trish. I will not ask you to work for free."

"Then don't ask. Consider me a volunteer."

THE NOTES WERE MUFFLED BUT DETECTABLE, LIKE the warbling of a woodland bird perched atop an evergreen, the pleasing trill floating on a mountain breeze.

The highly built-up storm had uneventfully rolled its way through Cedar Crest like a flash in the pan. Boom, and it was done. It did, however, deposit a fluffy padding of snow on the ground that wrapped around Samantha's boots like a slushy hug when she stepped onto her welcome mat.

Oliver was an early riser. Not much had changed there. He was up and out the door even before Samantha's alarm had buzzed. She was thankful for that small mercy. Oliver wasn't all bad. He wasn't even mostly bad. But his presence last night had tossed a monkey wrench straight into her wonderful evening with Noah. Samantha would be lying if she said there wasn't a little residual resentment tied to that.

Today was a new day. Fresh start. She'd give Oliver the clean slate he was due.

"Morning, Samantha." David looked up from his shoveling efforts a few yards away. There were several distinct paths leading throughout the cabin area, cleared walkways carved throughout last night's snow. Samantha figured this kindness was all his doing. "Headed to breakfast?"

"I am." She wound her cranberry hued scarf around her neck in two loose loops and tucked the fringed edges into her jacket collar. "Thank you so much for clearing all of this out of the way."

David shrugged like it was nothing, but the ruddy cheeks and fine sheen of sweat on his brow hinted otherwise. "Don't want anyone slipping. Plus, I enjoy shoveling. Always have. It's how I used to get my allowance as a kid. Back then, I got paid a penny per foot of snow I could shovel before sunrise. Took awhile to add up at that meager rate, but I usually ended up with a pretty heavy piggy bank by the end of the season."

"I love that. So many traditions around here." She ran her hands up and down her arms to generate some warmth. "Is that your mother I hear on the piano?"

"Marty, actually. Mom's headed into town with Grandma Kitty to pick up some groceries for the rest of the week. Vera's manning the dining hall this morning, but I've made her promise to take the afternoon off so she can rest up for her big day tomorrow." David propped the shovel in front of him and leaned forward on the handle. "Thank you for setting that up, by the way. I can't tell you how excited she is to do this commercial. She used to have dreams of being a big Hollywood star when she was a little girl, if you can believe it. Those aspirations have obviously changed over the years, but it's fun to see her fulfill that wish, even if it's on a smaller scale."

Samantha obviously hadn't been privy to Vera's childhood dreams, but that news was glorious music to her ears, just like the faint piano notes in the distance. The deal she'd arranged with Oliver—introducing him to Vera in exchange for one day of the crew's time—wasn't as above-board as she'd liked. She rarely did business in that sort of fashion, but desperate times called for equally desperate measures.

"I'm so happy to hear she's excited about the opportunity."

"Excited? She's about ready to pop—and that's not a pregnancy joke!" David gripped the handle of the shovel and scraped the thin metal ridge along the ground. Snow folded into it like a frosty accordion. "Anyway, I won't keep you. You should probably head on into breakfast before it gets cleaned up and put away. Vera's in nesting mode right now—nothing is safe."

"Will do. See you later, David."

Noah's younger brother tipped his head and Samantha scurried off, following his advice. She'd taken her sweet time this morning and her rumbling stomach made known its disapproval.

"Mornin', Sammy." Jack waved his daughter into the hall. He sat next to Joan, two empty plates positioned before them and a fully loaded one placed at the vacant seat next to him. "Made you a plate. All your favorites. Pancakes. Sausage. And I doused everything in about a pint of maple syrup, just the way you like it."

The exaggeration wasn't far off. Golden syrup drizzled across each breakfast item, glazing it with a sweetness Samantha could already taste on the tip of her tongue.

"Ah, thank you, Dad. I appreciate that."

She flopped down next to him and unfolded the cloth napkin to drape across her lap.

"Sweetie." Joan bent forward, her hands cupped around a half-empty mug of coffee, red nails clicking the ceramic. "Is there a reason Oliver is here?"

Jack gave his wife a look. "I thought we agreed we weren't going to broach that subject until *after* she had a full belly."

It was well known in their family that Samantha often got what some would label 'hangry' when she went too long between meals. That wasn't the issue in this scenario, but she chuckled at her parents' perceptiveness all the same.

"I can talk while I eat." Spearing a link of sausage with the tines of her fork, Samantha lifted it to her mouth and made eye contact with her mom. "I know Oliver's here."

"You invited him?"

Mothers were inclined to dislike their ex-son-in-laws, but Samantha knew Joan had a difficult time mustering that up regarding Oliver. He was charming, especially with the senior population of females, for whatever reason. And the divorce hadn't been in response to an adulterous affair or unsavory, vengeful act. They'd parted ways because they truly never should have joined together to begin with. The fault rested on both sets of shoulders.

Joan liked Oliver, always had and probably always would. Jack, on the other hand, was not quiet about his disapproval. Samantha was her daddy's girl. That hedge of fatherly protection would always be wrapped around her, tight as a big bear hug.

"I didn't invite him. Not really, at least. He needed a pregnant woman for a project, and Vera came to mind. We worked it out so that we can use their camera crew for a day once they're finished filming their commercial. It's a win-win. Sort of."

Joan leaned in. "Do you think the Jensens even plan to make a commercial anymore?"

"I do. It's their only marketing strategy that I'm aware of right now."

"Sinterklaas left this morning, you know," Joan whispered like it was the town's juiciest gossip. "Hired for a feast on December sixth down in Sacramento. That only leaves us and Father Christmas. Even Mother Christmas already left town. I'm just not sure this is such a good idea anymore, sweetie. It feels a little like things are unraveling."

The two original reasons for Samantha's presence at the cabins sat beside to her, and if they chose to bow out of the running, then what was she to do?

"You're not planning to go, too, are you?"

"No." Jack was fast with his answer. "We're not going anywhere."

He covered his daughter's hand with his huge palm. Jack's hands were bigger than any man's Samantha had ever seen, almost like paws. As a little girl, her entire fist could curl up in his, smothered like a massive glove around her tiny fingers. She knew all daddies were larger than life; heroes in their own right. But Jack justly deserved that title, especially after everything he went through with Seth so many years ago.

"We're seeing this through, Sammy," Jack avowed in true, fatherly form. "You have my word."

Samantha smiled weakly and took another bite. Back home, she wasn't much of a breakfast eater. It was typically a grab-and-go sort of deal, and often just a cup of coffee from her favorite shop was enough to propel her day in the right direction. But her mother's confession unmoored her. She buried that confusion under bite after bite of food.

"I'm working on a script as we speak." The fib was palpably bitter on her tongue. Samantha chased it with a sugary, syrup-drenched mouthful of pancakes. "Should have it done by tomorrow evening, in fact. Don't worry, you two. I've got everything handled. Get your best Mr. and Mrs. Claus impressions ready. It's almost go time!"

$\mathcal{N}$oah could've walked in on Santa's eight reindeer dancing the cha-cha and he couldn't've possibly been more dumbfounded.

He was good about things like half-yearly visits to the dentist and he routinely changed out the oil in his car. The one thing he didn't keep up with was getting his eyes checked. Always had twenty-twenty vision, so far as he could tell. But right now, his eyes deceived him; he was positive about that.

Marty and Samantha sat shoulder-to-shoulder at the baby grand piano. Under her hand was a spiral notebook placed upright on the music rack, and the pen gripped within her fingers flew over the lines like a frenzied dog chasing a squirrel. While she wrote, his brother plunked out notes in a choppy, yet cheerful, couplet that had hints of holiday appeal.

When they were kids, Marty would spend hours at that wooden bench, nestled up against their mother's side, memorizing the sound each note produced when she struck a certain key or chord. Sometimes, Noah almost thought Marty would be the sort to run away and join a grunge band. There was a God-given talent there, even if it was suppressed under teenage angst and indifference most of the time. Every once in a while, though, Marty would surprise them all and push back the piano's fallboard, using his gifted hands as the worthy instruments they were.

Everyone was careful not to dole out accolades. If they became too complimentary, Marty would snap back into his shell like a clam, shutting off and shutting them out. Noah paid heed to this knowledge and slowly approached the duo at the opposite end of the room.

"Noah!" Samantha's hand froze mid-scribble. She beckoned him with a waving gesture. "You have to listen to this!"

"It's not ready." Like old, frustrating times, Marty slammed the lid and shoved back.

"But it's close. A work in progress, if you will."

"I'm going to get something to eat." Without so much as polite eye contact, Marty stormed past Noah in an aggravated blur. "We can work on it later."

Mouth pinched, Samantha's shoulders sank. She tapped her lips with the eraser end of her pencil. "I still haven't quite figured him out."

"You and me both!" Noah let out a massive guffaw that bent him at the waist. "Don't take it personally. He's like that with everyone."

"He's not so bad, really. And he's a genius when it comes to the piano."

"Genius?" Noah's eyebrows shot into his hairline. "You sure about that?"

"I'm not kidding. He's more talented than a lot of the musicians I work with. He has an ear for music that's so natural, so effortless. You can't teach that sort of thing—you either have it or you don't."

"Do you mind me asking what exactly it is that the two of you were working on?"

"A jingle," she offered. "For your commercial."

"That's not something you need to—"

"I know it's not something I *need* to do. It's something I *want* to do. And oddly enough, it's something your brother was actually willing to help me with, so there's that."

"Well, you can be pretty convincing."

"Is that so?" Samantha's lips hooked into a coquettish smirk.

"You convinced me a life of unending bachelorhood might not be as appealing as it once was," Noah confessed freely. "And you also convinced me it was okay to muster up the courage to kiss you."

"I don't think there was any convincing needed there. That was completely mutual," she said. "But if you do need convincing in the future, I'd be happy to persuade you."

"Are you flirting with me, Samantha?"

"I might be. I don't know. I'm woefully out of practice."

"You can practice on me anytime you'd like. Same goes for the kissing part." Noah took his position next to her on the bench and bumped her shoulder with his. "In all seriousness, I'm glad you're still here, doing this." He waved his hand over the pages of notes propped up in front of them. "It means a lot that you believe in this place enough to put in the time to help us get back on track."

"I *do* believe in this place. I believe in you. And I also believe in the magic of Christmas," she said. "I'm biased and still think my parents are going to be the best fit for the commercial once we have one, but I know that's not my decision."

"Seeing that we're down to just two candidates even interested in sticking around, I'd say they have a pretty decent chance," Noah said. He met her gaze and held it, wondering if he should ask his next question. "So, I know it's none of my business, but I take it things went okay with Oliver last night?"

"Yep. I haven't even seen him today. Vera said your mom got him set up with his own room this morning and my guess is he's knee-deep in work. I know I'm not the best at taking a vacation, but that man is even worse, if you can believe it."

"You're both driven. I'm sure that's why you've been able to run a successful agency for so many years."

"That's part of it, but the talent we represent is what really keeps us running. Without our clients, we wouldn't have much of a business to speak of."

Noah half laughed. "Sort of like a mountain lodge with no guests."

"We're going to find you those guests, Noah. They're out there, they just need to know you are, too."

This inspiring woman at his side had also been out there, and yet he'd been unaware of her existence until just a few short days ago. That thought sat with him as they continued bantering, falling into easy conversation like old friends.

Things could change in a moment. Hearts could open. Hope could flourish.

Heck, even Marty could take to the keys and compose again. Miracles abounded, even if in the tiniest of forms.

"Any chance you're free tonight? I know you and my brother have plans to work on the jingle later, but if I could steal you for an hour or so, there's somewhere I'd like to take you."

Samantha's eyes sparkled with amusement, and her mouth spread into a slow, pleased grin. "You know what, Noah Jensen? I think I could probably be *convinced* to do that."

IF HIS MEMORY SERVED HIM CORRECTLY, HE'D FIND what he was looking for in the old woodshop behind the cabins, hanging on the wall immediately to the left of the rickety door. The only people to ever really use them were his dad and grandpa. Snowshoes weren't the most stylish footwear, and as boys, Noah and his brothers enjoyed sinking clear up to their knees in loose snow when they traipsed around the property, anyway. David had teased that the shoes looked like tennis rackets and Noah almost wondered now if that would be a good backup option if he couldn't locate the snowshoes.

"I'm not going to ask Samantha to wear actual tennis rackets on her feet," he scolded himself aloud, headshake and all. "That's just ridiculous."

Thankfully, he didn't have to entertain that silly option for long. Like vintage décor in a ski chalet, two pairs of snowshoes adorned the wall right where he remembered them, each set crossing one over the other to create what resembled two hearts.

"Thanks, guys." Noah directed his eyes heavenward with gratitude and smiled.

He'd never brought a woman home to meet his parents—never really dated anyone long enough that it seemed appropriate to do so. But he knew his dad would have adored Samantha. He'd good naturedly rib her about her given name, teasing her like she was one of the family. Andy Jensen had a way of doing that, bringing people into the fold with ease and effortless ability. Was that something Noah inherited from him? He sure hoped so. Of all of his father's legacies, that was the greatest—to make people feel welcome, just as they were. To Noah it was, at least.

He slipped the shoes off their hooks, one at a

time, then lowered them to the workbench in the center of the room. Sawdust remained on the surface of the old table, remnants from projects completed years earlier. A tear crept into Noah's eye—just in the corner of one—and he wondered how the mere thought of leftover dust could reduce him that way. But he could feel his dad and grandpa in this space, more than any other place on their property. It was the only landscape that didn't change, mostly because it had remained largely untouched since their passing.

Flower bulbs would go into the ground in the planters come springtime. New shrubs and ground-cover. The cabins would even get a fresh coat of stain. Linens weren't purchased seasonally like they used to be back in busier times, but as frequent as yearly now. Grandma Kitty would add new items and dishes to the menu. Perhaps Audrey would even compose a new song to serenade future guests.

There was so much newness, even in the midst of carrying on tradition.

But the woodshop—in there it was as though time had paused right along with his father and grandfather's lives. Because that's what it was; a pause. There would be a time when they would all be reunited. That truth sustained Noah. It sustained their whole family.

Taking the snowshoes from the table, the rounded edge of one caught a lip on a nearby box lid. The cardboard lifted, then toppled over. Sawdust plumed and scattered, causing Noah's throat to tickle with an impending cough.

"What is that?" He moved closer.

Nestled within the box was a pile of carved wooden toys. Noah's breath caught. His hand dove into the box of its own volition, fishing around and withdrawing figurine after figurine. He lined them up like soldiers on the workbench. Toy trains—a caboose and a railcar, to be exact. A whittled horse. A miniature baseball bat sculpted from a longer piece of alder wood. Even a working nutcracker, complete with handle and unhinged jaw.

These were the toys of his childhood and the ones his father and grandfather had created for Santa to hand out to their guests on Christmas morning. When Grandma Kitty had recalled their history, it hadn't occurred to Noah that these might exist: ungifted toys. He thought of his father tucking them away, tucking his original dreams for the cabins away along with them.

That wasn't going to work for Noah. Not while he had the capacity to fulfill those unrealized wishes.

Christmas at Cedar Crest Cabins would be different from the last couple of years. If there was one thing Noah could guarantee, it was that plain and simple fact.

CHAPTER 19

When Samantha was a young girl, she and her brother, Seth, would often raid their parents' closets on slow Sunday mornings. They would drape themselves in clothing countless sizes too big and shoes that mimicked flippers on their small feet. After adorning herself in heavy-handed makeup and gobs of costume jewelry that belonged on a garage sale folding table rather than on a young girl, she would fasten a proud smile to her lips and steady herself along the wall with her hands. If she didn't take this precaution, she'd teeter and topple as she made her way toward her parents in the family room. They always played along with her little fashion shows, faces beaming with an enthusiasm Samantha now recognized as parental love.

They were so amenable, much like Noah, who currently acted as though it didn't bother him one bit to have Samantha clinging to his arm while bumbling across the wintery terrain.

"They take some time to get used to." His gloved hand moved to wrap around her waist and keep her upright. "You'll get the hang of it. But if you don't, I'm completely happy to hold on to you. In fact, I sort of hope you *don't* get the hang of it."

Samantha warmed even though she'd already worked up a sweat beneath her parka. Snowshoeing was about as fun as running on a sandy beach. It required a stamina Samantha hadn't built up yet. She knew some people favored that sort of exercise, but such things didn't motivate her.

What did motivate her was the surprise Noah said awaited them on that mountain crest. Before they'd left, she spent more time at the piano with Marty, but her thoughts weren't attached to that work. Instead, she kept dreaming of what the evening might possibly hold.

Was there some sort of romantic, candlelit picnic decorating the snow-capped peak? Rose petals and a bottle of vintage wine? She doubted it. The wind was rough, and a single gust would extinguish the flames and send the flowers scattering like snowflakes. Still, the thought of a secluded dinner made her heart patter.

Maybe a sleigh ride? She hadn't seen any horses around the property, and if there had been a barn filled with animals, one of the Jensens would be tasked with caring for them. As far as she could tell, that wasn't the case.

A few other ideas entered and left her mind, each one making her brim with giddiness. It didn't matter what the surprise might be. All that mattered was that she would be with Noah. He could take her up the mountain, say absolutely nothing, and turn around to hike back down, and it would still be a lovely evening. Just being in his presence was enough for her. Being at his side. Holding his hand.

If he had been alone, Samantha figured the trek would've been completed in half the time. She apologized more than she needed to for lagging behind. Noah wouldn't have it. There was no place for apologies on this hike; the journey was part of the process.

"We're getting close," he assured when it felt like Samantha's knees might buckle and drop her into the snowpack in an exhausted heap. "Just over the ridge."

So far, her time at Cedar Crest had been spent around the cabins, moving in and out of the dining hall, visiting with her parents, or enjoying the views from her cabin window. There was a great beyond she hadn't had the chance to discover.

It felt almost trite in the way well-loved songs became rote and routine, but the words from *Winter Wonderland* served as a fitting narrative for their twilight excursion up the mountainside.

Glistening snow. Chilled nose. It was indeed a beautiful sight, and to say that Samantha was happy was an understatement. She couldn't recall the last time she'd been so filled with joy.

"Almost there."

With a final push, Samantha mustered her energy to climb the last several feet of elevation. She could see the crest ahead and the horizon it created as sheer, unblemished white met the navy sky above.

"Just over here."

Noah moved quicker now, and Samantha fought to match his pace. He released her and slung his backpack around to his middle. Inside was a rolled up wool blanket and a stainless steel Thermos. He indicated for her to sit on a huge felled log and then took his place next to her, draping the heavy fabric across their legs.

It struck Samantha as odd that she felt the juxtaposition of two temperatures, both hot and cold, in the same moment. There was the flush of exertion, but an equal chill that took hold when the icy air caressed her exposed cheeks and skin.

"Take a minute to catch your breath," Noah suggested sweetly. He unscrewed the cap to the Thermos.

There was no use pretending she was in better shape than she was. Her sad struggle was glaringly evident. "You must think I'm a couch potato. I swear, I'm not usually this winded."

"It's the altitude. Air's thinner up here. A lot of people forget about that."

"Well, I'll take any excuse I can get. Yes, it's totally

the altitude and not my laziness showing." She laughed at her own absurdity and swept her hair from her face with the back of her hand. "Do you get used to it?"

"Seeing that I've never lived anywhere else, I never had to get used to it. But people do. If you spend enough time here, the elevation isn't so noticeable." His chin lifted, eyes following. "But there are some perks to being this high up."

Samantha let her gaze linger on the man next to her for a greedy moment. The sun had set hours earlier, but nature had its own way of lighting up the dark. The sheet of snow beneath them and the crescent moon above reflected just enough to swath Noah's strong profile in soft, diffused light. There was a scruffiness to his jaw that hadn't been there when they'd first met. A few days without a good shave was enough to turn him into a certified mountain man in the very best way.

He caught her. "Hey, what are you looking at?" His mouth pricked up in the corner.

"You."

"When you could look at this?" He gestured toward the starry firmament above them.

"I have the rest of my life to look at the night sky." Samantha's hand moved over the blanket to touch his knee. "I only have one week to appreciate this particular view."

Noah's throat worked on a swallow that bobbed his Adam's apple. He didn't answer, but she knew she hadn't asked a question. Still, there was a little testing of the waters going on. Maybe she had hoped he'd say it wouldn't be over at the end of the week. That they could see where life took things. See if their relationship was worth the distance between them.

She didn't speak for several minutes, giving him the space to deliver that hoped-for response. It didn't come.

"You know we're big on tradition around here," Noah said finally, changing the subject just like Samantha suspected he would.

She couldn't let that disappoint her. It wasn't entirely fair to cue him up in that way and then be frustrated when she didn't get the result she had wanted. She'd have to let it go.

"Grandma Kitty let you in on a few," Noah continued, "but there's one I haven't shared."

He poured the contents of the Thermos into two tin mugs, the type Samantha's parents had packed away with their camping gear.

"Peppermint white mocha?" Samantha couldn't believe her taste buds. "How did you manage that?"

"With an internet recipe and a little of Grandma Kitty's help. Oh, and Vera's, too. Apparently, one of her cravings has been white chocolate, so we had full bars of it stowed away in the kitchen." He paused. "One more thing." Dipping his hand into his backpack, he took out a canister of whipped cream. "Can't forget the best part."

"You are one of the most thoughtful men I've ever met, Noah."

He sprayed a towering swirl of the cream onto the surface of her drink. "Because I made you a cup of coffee?"

"Because you made me feel seen."

He halted.

"It's easy to notice the big things about a person, but the little stuff? Their preferences and likes? That stuff often flits in and out. It doesn't stick." She lapped at the whipped cream and savored the sweetness on her tongue.

"Everything about you sticks with me, Samantha." He held her gaze, then slipped his hand out of his glove. "You have a little something." Swiping at the tip of her nose, he chuckled when his finger came back with a dollop of whipped cream on it.

"Is it weird I'm not even embarrassed about my messy eating? This is just so yummy; I can't help myself." She swallowed down a mouthful of the holiday drink and sighed contentedly. "But I interrupted you. You were saying something about traditions?"

"I was, but it can wait while you enjoy that."

"I can multi-task. I can enjoy this *and* listen to you. Like walking and chewing gum."

"Or talking and snowshoeing," he chided.

"I was a little quiet on the way up here. I'll give you that. But that was all because I didn't want to fall and make an utter fool of myself. Or expend any extra energy. Snowshoeing uphill is not for the faint of heart."

"You're a good sport, Sam."

It was the first time he'd shortened her name in that endearing way and it warmed her more than the coffee.

"Anyway." His eyes angled heavenward again. "Back in our heyday, we had a lot of traditions around here. You know about the wooden gifts. Caroling around the piano. Things like that. But there's one I haven't told you, and it's probably what we're known for most." He took her free hand. "Unfortunately, I think we're mainly known for the tragedy that went along with it."

Noah's grip tightened around hers.

"I haven't told you how my dad and grandpa passed. It was a plane crash. Not a big commercial flight, but one of those light aircraft. Grandpa Paul was flying; Dad was co-pilot. That's how they usually did things," Noah started. "They were both experienced. Thousands of hours between the two of them. It was their passion. They loved flying almost as much as they loved these cabins."

Samantha moved to place her mug onto the log, then lowered her hand onto Noah's, cupping his between her two palms. "I'm so sorry, Noah. I know what it's like to lose a loved one. It's a pain completely unique unto itself."

"It's been a few years and I'm healing. Still grieving, but healing." He half smiled and sniffed. "They were taking a final test flight to make sure everything was ready for the big night."

"The big night?"

"Christmas Eve," he said. "Every year they would fly over the cabins right around midnight."

She couldn't understand why they would want to be out at that late hour the night before such an important holiday. Samantha's favorite part was always heading to bed early so she could wake up even sooner to discover the stack of presents beneath the tree. Even as an adult, there wasn't much better than a cozy, full night's sleep on Christmas Eve.

"When I was little—back before I stopped believing—I honestly thought it was Santa's sleigh with his eight reindeer," he continued. "That blinking red strobe on their plane had me convinced Rudolph was at the helm. Convinced all the other kids, too." Noah's shoulders lifted with a large inhale. His breath left him in a frozen cloud that hovered a few feet out. "Even when our numbers were low and we didn't have any guests—any children, at least—Dad and Grandpa would still do their fly over. I think they were doing it just for us boys at that point. But it was always magical. Even as a teenager, I'd sometimes forget it was them up there and not Santa himself."

"What a beautiful tradition, Noah. I'm so sorry it had to end so tragically."

"I go back and forth between thinking it was such an unfair way for them to die and believing it's how they would have wanted to go. Doing something they loved. People always say that, right? 'At least they died doing something they loved.' To be honest, Dad and Grandpa loved everything about this mountain ridge they called home."

He cleared his throat and pushed the heel of his hand to his cheek, likely hoping to smother the tears before Samantha could notice them. But his vulnerability laid bare, and she'd never felt closer to the man next to her than in that moment. Her heart constricted with a familiar ache for him.

"They sacrificed their lives for this place, Samantha," he said. "I used to think it was my duty to make sure these cabins survived. Now I recognize it's my honor."

CHAPTER 20

They sat side by side and talked about life and loss as nightfall settled around them. Clouds silently moved in, releasing a trickle of snow that stuck to Samantha's eyelashes and dusted her shoulders with little white flakes. She'd placed her head on Noah's shoulder. They shared a kiss. He felt himself falling in love.

The next morning, Noah woke with peace in his heart. Samantha had plans with Marty, but they enjoyed breakfast together beforehand. He teased her about her excessive use of syrup and she poked fun at the way he delicately held his fork like a pencil.

"Better than a shovel," he'd teased. "I'm no Neanderthal, Sam."

He had to be careful or he could all too easily envision a future like this: sharing a meal and his life with this woman.

It's what he wanted. He'd never wanted anything

more. Some would say it was too early to tell, but it didn't feel that way with Samantha. She was the missing puzzle piece finally discovered and locking into place.

Oliver was hard at work with Vera and an assortment of other actors that arrived in a caravan of SUVs and trucks a little after dawn. Noah had spent little time with Marty's production crew, but he quickly realized that they had been a ramshackle operation when compared to Oliver's team. Today there were light booms and microphones with fuzzy covers and bulky cameras with lenses that looked as heavy as dumbbells. It was the real deal.

Vera had been a bundle of butterflies, and David tried and failed to talk her off the ledge multiple times. But once Oliver swept in and assured her she was born to be a star—even if only in a canned soup commercial—that apprehension dissolved.

Oliver was charming, Noah could credit him that much. His presence was commanding and authoritative, but he also knew how to amp up the charisma when required. For most of the morning, Oliver sat back and let the director do her thing, but he maintained a watchful gaze from the sidelines, arms crossed and brow strained tight above scrutinizing eyes.

Noah knew they didn't need more cooks in the kitchen, so he ducked out of the way and meandered to the woodshed around noon. Last night's discovery remained on the workbench, each figure on display like it belonged in a small-town toyshop. Noah picked up the nutcracker and ran his thumb over the recessed details.

It was the work of a master carpenter. Tipping it upside down, he noticed the letters *AJ* impressed on the base of the figure. This particular one had been his father's creation. Moving through the remaining toys, he separated those carved by his dad from the ones his grandfather had crafted. The artistry was relatively indistinguishable, both men equally artistic in bringing these pieces to life from a block of wood.

What Noah wouldn't give for the opportunity to be under their tutelage. He was handy by nature. He liked to fix things and tinker around. But he'd been young when they stopped making these wooden gifts for their guests. He didn't have the privilege of pulling up a chair to watch as his dad whittled away the unnecessary portions of scrap wood to reveal a masterpiece trapped within the timber. He didn't witness the process. In truth, he grieved a little over that.

It took Noah some time to reacquaint himself with the layout of the shed. He imagined its door hadn't even been opened in recent years. Not until last night, at least. Even so, all the necessary tools were still in their respective places. He gathered the gauge and the chisel and found his dad's old mallet close by. He shouldn't've been surprised to uncover a small stack of pre-cut wood blocks, but the discovery made his chest tighten all the same.

Hiking a leg up onto a stool, Noah took a block in one hand and the chisel into the other. Fine curls of shaved wood fell to the table with each swipe of the knife. He sanded and smoothed all while humming carols quietly under his breath. It was the best sort of therapy, to be doing something his dad loved in a place he felt most at home. Noah felt closer to him than he had in a long while.

There might've been a knock, but Noah didn't hear it. His focus was so narrowed, the outside world almost ceased to exist.

"Hope I'm not interrupting." Jack Day's voice and figure cut through Noah's concentration. He crossed into the small shed to come over to Noah's side.

Noah lowered his carving to the table and picked up a rag to dust off his hands. "Not at all. How's it going, Jack?"

"Can't complain, can't complain," Jack answered. He looked around. "This is quite the little woodshop you've got here."

"It actually belonged to my dad and my grandpa." Noah ran a hand across his brow, surprised he'd worked up a sweat. "I don't really know what I'm doing. Just playing around."

Jack eyed the piece of wood. "Looks to me like you know a little something." He picked it up and rotated it in his palm before returning it back to the table. "Mind if I hide out in here for a bit? The little girl playing Vera's daughter in the commercial just spotted Father Christmas and I worry if she sees me too, it'll cause some confusion."

"Can't have two Santas running loose at the cabins."

Jack chuckled heartily. "Never heard of Santa Claus having a twin."

"You're more than welcome to hang out in here as long as you like, Jack. I'd enjoy the company."

"Speaking of company, I hear you've been enjoying my daughter's lately."

Noah's throat went dry.

Jack held up a reassuring hand. "I'm just giving you a hard time, Noah. Couldn't be more delighted to see the two of you hitting it off. Samantha deserves someone like you. Someone who values her and treats her well. Don't get me wrong. Oliver is a fine enough man, but his ego is sometimes bigger than his heart."

The unexpected compliment caught Noah off guard. "Your approval means a lot, sir."

"Ah, don't go getting all formal with me now. I'm casual about this sort of thing. If Sammy's happy, I'm happy. And trust me, I've never seen her happier," Jack noted. "You've brought something out of her that's been buried a long time."

"She does the same for me."

"I'm glad to hear it. I know we don't know each other all that well yet, but I'm a decent judge of character. From what I can see, yours is as good as it gets."

"That's high praise," Noah acknowledged. "Praise I'm not entirely sure I deserve."

"I find the people who resist compliments are often the ones that deserve them the most." Jack nodded knowingly. "Humility is a lost trait these days. Glad to see you're bringing it back into fashion."

A friendship formed that afternoon in the woodshed. Jack was easy to talk with, fun to be around. Noah glimpsed pieces of Samantha in her father's mannerisms and his attentive nature. He listened well and interjected leading questions, which kept the conversation lively and interesting. Jack even tried his hand at carving, but soon found his Santa skills were limited in that area.

"Don't tell my daughter," he said. "I've got her fooled into thinking I'm the best Santa Claus there is this side of the North Pole."

"She's not wrong. You're jolly, spirited, and—"

"If you say fat, I'm going to take back all of those nice things I said about you earlier." Jack shook a finger.

"I was going to say generous."

"Well, jeez. That's really nice." Jack snickered to himself. "I suppose I've got a generous waistline, too. All in the name of authenticity."

It was nearing dusk when David came to find them.

"Production's all wrapped up," he said as the trio walked back for dinner. The air was cool and the sky, cloudless. "Vera was amazing today, but I expected nothing less. She really fell right into her role. Memorized her lines like a pro." David propped the door open with his boot and allowed the other men to go through first. "And the team left us with a pallet of canned chicken noodle soup as a bonus. It's got nothing on Grandma Kitty's, but it'll do."

Tonight, they shoved the tables together and broke bread as a family would. Even Oliver joined them, though he was quieter than Noah expected him to be. Maybe the day had taken it out of him the way it had clearly exhausted poor Vera. She sat close to David in her chair, her body slumped against his, eyelids fluttering shut every few minutes.

Halfway through the meal, Samantha excused herself to retrieve a bottle of champagne from her cabin, citing the night as one of celebration. Noah couldn't help but notice the way Oliver's gaze tracked her from across the room. How his eyes remained trained on the door even once she was on the other side of it.

Samantha had said the split was mutual, but nothing about Oliver's attentiveness corroborated that. There was love in his gaze, and if it wasn't love, at the very least, it was longing.

"Oliver," Jack addressed as the plates were being cleared. "I hear things went well today."

Side conversations had formed in groups of twos and threes, but Noah didn't join.

"That's the consensus," Oliver replied. He fiddled with the rolled collar of his turtleneck sweater. "My actors are happy. The production company and film crew seem to be, too. That, of course, makes me happy." He took hold of the thin stem of his wine-glass and gave it a mindless swirl. "And tomorrow morning we'll be back at it again."

"Noah, did you settle on a script for the commercial?" Jack inquired.

Though Noah tried to remain on the sidelines of the discussion, Jack didn't appear to get that memo.

"Samantha and Marty are handling things in that department," he said.

"So what is it exactly that *you* do?" Oliver finally used the wineglass for more than twirling and raised it to his lips. He sucked in a liberal sip and swished like mouthwash before swallowing it down, but his blink-less gaze challenged Noah's.

"Noah owns a handyman company." Grandma Kitty's palms landed proudly on her grandson's shoulders when she came up from behind. She leaned over to collect his empty plate and water cup. "Comfort Valley Repair Resource. You heard of it?"

"Can't say I have."

That was fair. It wasn't as though Noah had heard of Oliver's talent agency before this week. Their worlds were so different; they didn't even seem to share the same atmosphere.

"Does that keep you pretty busy?"

"It does."

"Lots of things in need of repair in this town?" Oliver implied in a haughty tone that made Noah bristle. "Things around you falling apart?"

"Lots of things needing attention to ensure they

don't fall apart. That's usually the best way to do it. From my experience, at least."

Noah no longer referred to his business or even the little town in general, but he reckoned Oliver hadn't picked up on that subtlety. Why would he? Oliver's failed marriage with Samantha was none of Noah's business. And yet Noah felt thrown into the middle of those tumultuous emotions, as if he could somehow right past hurts by defending Samantha's honor in the here and now.

"I enjoy what I do." Noah got his feelings—and his head—back on track. "I enjoy the people I get to work with."

"Enjoying the people you work with makes all the difference in the world." The slyest of winks flickered just one eye. "I, for one, can vouch for that."

CHAPTER 21

*I*f she hadn't known better, Samantha would've been tempted to look over her shoulder, if only to make sure someone wasn't physically pushing her. The wind was that forceful, that gusty and downright rude.

The layout of the property usually made for a brisk walk between buildings—a walk she had slogged countless times—but in the stretch it took Samantha to trudge from the dining room to Cabin #8, Mother Nature kicked her attitude up several notches. Snow no longer fell, but sailed sideways and diagonally and even in cyclone swirls. Slushy flakes marred Samantha's vision in wet, fat clumps.

And the wind. It howled like a desperate wolf separated from the pack, shrieking with feral tenacity in her ears as it whipped and whirled through the mountains.

When she'd located the champagne bottle back in

the cabin, the lamp on her nightstand and the cords twisted around the tree flickered a warning, as if to say their cooperation wasn't fully guaranteed. That omen didn't sit well with Samantha. For as resilient as she gave herself credit, she was no prairie woman. Power wasn't a luxury in her book, but a requirement she'd come to expect.

When she finally tumbled into the dining hall, out of breath and even a little disgruntled, the entirety of the room looked at her, saucer-wide eyes blinking and stunned.

"Sammy!" Jack jumped from his seat. Noah wasn't far behind. "Sweetie, are you okay?"

"I think I found that big storm the meteorologists have been talking about all week. It's angry out there."

Wind clapped upon the shutters like an icy smack. Samantha jerked. She wasn't often afraid of a storm, but this one had ugly plans. She could sense it in her bones.

"The lights flickered back at the cabin," she informed.

"In here, too," Noah affirmed. "Just a quick blip, but I don't imagine we'll get through this without losing power."

"I should probably head back to my cabin." Oliver stood. "Before that option is off the table."

"I'd advise against that." Marty's arms were bound tightly over his chest, his feet kicked up on a chair opposite him, boots crossed at the ankles. He shook his head knowingly. "Best to ride this one out in here."

"Why would I do that when my cabin is just down the hill?"

"Because this is where we keep the bulk of the food," David reasoned. "There's a large fireplace and several cords of tarped wood along the outside wall of the building." He spoke at a hushed volume so he didn't wake his wife slumbering peacefully against his shoulder, but he didn't come across any less resolute. "And if the power's out and this storm turns out to be as bad as it feels like it has the potential to be, then you don't want to be trapped in a frigid, little cabin. Trust me."

"You've done this a time or two?" Samantha assumed.

"Or three or four," Noah said. "I agree with my brothers. We should all stay put. I know I'd feel better knowing we're all under one roof, anyway."

"What about the film crew?" Samantha sat down at the table. Worry had already taken root and she couldn't shake it. She twisted a napkin in her hands.

"They're staying at Sierra Elevations down the road," Oliver chimed in, like it was the best news in the world. "Lined them up with a few luxury suites over there. They should be just fine."

She was sure it was said in an attempt to flex his planning skills and possibly even his corporate card, but Samantha's face flamed. "You're kidding, right?

Were you not aware that there are perfectly good cabins for rent right here?"

"Cabins I assumed were already occupied by a hoard of Santa Clauses," Oliver disputed.

It was a fair assumption, even the right one, but the way Oliver delivered the information was true to form. He knew best, or at least carried an air of pretention that made it come across that way.

"Go with the red dress," he'd said their last Christmas together when she'd vacillated over which fancy cocktail dress to wear to dinner with his parents. *"You always wear green because you think it compliments your eyes, but it makes your skin tone look a little sickly. Red really brightens you up."*

It was no coincidence her favorite item of clothing in her current closet was her emerald coat. He wasn't privy to her feelings, but it was very near an act of rebellion in her mind each time she shrugged it onto her shoulders. It was as close to telling him off as she'd ever get, if only in the form of women's attire.

Oliver's opinions should hold little weight in her life. Yet there was still a niggling feeling that scratched at her, like an itch she couldn't quite reach. They were coworkers and partners and, for whatever reason, she wanted to impress him. Make him proud in some silly way. Because he wasn't a bad man. He had a heart under his designer sweaters. A heart she knew so very well.

"I'm going to put a few kettles on while we still have power. I'll bring everyone a filled Thermos and you can use the hot water to make cider or cocoa, whichever you prefer." Audrey pressed back from the table.

Joan stood, too. "I'll join you."

"And I'll gather the table linens from the storage closet," Kitty offered, shuffling right behind the two women. "Might not be as cozy as heavy blankets or quilts, but if we lose power and the temperature drops, I don't think anyone will complain about warming up under a tablecloth."

Samantha felt helpless and a little untethered, unsure what the best use of her time or talents might be.

"I should go with them," she said to Noah, looking for verification.

"I'm sure they've got things handled." He took her hand. "But I could use some help with the fire, if you're up for that."

"I'm willing to help out in any way I can."

"Good. Then follow me."

On the other side of the room, just a few paces from the swinging doors leading into the kitchen, was a stately stone fireplace, the massive sort that stretched floor to ceiling. It had a chunky wooden mantle wide enough for hanging at least a dozen stockings, maybe more. Soot stained the inside of the hearth and evidence of use tinged the ceiling above a gray, smoky hue.

It was clearly trusty and dependable, and Samantha was grateful for that. She'd been chilled on her walk and had yet to warm up. A fire would alleviate that. So would being snuggled up to the man next to her, but she didn't let her mind dwell on that particularly enticing thought for too long.

Noah stacked the logs and Samantha crumpled torn pieces of newspaper for kindling. It became evident that he needed little help in the effort, but she was glad he'd requested her aid all the same. He picked up a metal canister and held it out at arm's length.

She took the container, popped off the lid, and pulled out a long matchstick to strike against the side. The rough end of the match blazed to life, reminding her of the sparklers she loved from Fourth of July celebrations.

"Go ahead. It's all you." Noah nudged his chin toward the pile of cut lumber and shredded newsprint.

Samantha bent forward. Flames crawled over the papers and the wood, growing in height and warmth as they ignited the elements in their path.

"Would you believe that's the first real fire I've ever started?" She felt oddly proud, even though it wasn't a monumental feat. "I've always just flipped on a switch, which feels a little like cheating now that I've done this."

"I thought you've had a fire going in the cabin."

"I have, but I might've enlisted my dad's help for that. Don't tell anyone."

Noah chuckled. "Your secret's safe with me."

Samantha rocked back from her crouched position to sit fully on the floor. Folding her legs up beneath her, she stared into the flames. "Should we be worried?" she asked, scolding the tremble out of her voice. "About the storm?"

"Worry has never added an hour to a man's life, so no, I don't think there's any sense in worrying about the things we can't control." Noah joined her on the hardwood. He reached out and slipped a wayward strand of her hair behind her ear in a gesture that felt intimate and appreciated. "Not if you can help it, at least."

"That's the problem. I don't think I *can* help it. My mind flits to these worst-case scenarios and I can feel myself start to spiral. Once that starts, it's hard to stop."

"I understand that." He scooted closer so they were shoulder to shoulder. "I think since our worst-case scenarios have happened—me with my dad and grandpa and you with your brother—it's not hard for our minds to conjure up other bad stuff. But I've tried to make a practice of shooting down those thoughts before they settle in and become full-fledged fears," he said. "I try to see the good that can come out of something bad. Because it's always there. Sometimes it's hidden, but it's always there."

Samantha drew her knees to her chest and wrapped her arms around her legs in a hug. "I haven't told you much about my brother, but I think his story is something you should know."

"Only if you're comfortable. Don't feel like you have to just because I shared with you last night."

"No, no. I want to tell you. It'll explain a few things," she said, nodding to herself. "Like how I ended up with Oliver."

Noah did a decent job masking the surprise Samantha knew was there. He kept his mouth in a line and his eyes trained on hers. "I would be honored to hear anything you're willing to share with me."

She took a breath, held it in her lungs to the point of stinging, and then pushed it out in a rush. "I mentioned briefly that my brother had spent some time at the Children's Hospital. It was a car crash, a brutal one. He was in a coma and he never came out of it."

"Oh, Samantha…"

"He wasn't the only one involved. His best friend, Taylor, had been driving and suffered the brunt of the physical trauma. So many broken bones. I can't even tell you how many surgeries that poor kid endured," she said. "But Taylor was a fighter, just like my brother. They both fought so hard, Noah. Even still, in the end, neither of them made it out of that hospital."

She took another breath before continuing.

"It was right before Christmas and my mom and dad were doing their Santa gig there. That meant I was their resident elf. I'll admit, it wasn't my favorite seasonal job, especially since I was a high school senior. And I had already spent so much time at that hospital. But there was a cute boy right around my age who was also a patient. We flirted, and he poked fun at me in a really endearing way. But his heart was failing, had been since he was twelve. And we knew there was a good chance he wouldn't make it to Christmas."

"Oliver?" Noah inferred.

Samantha nodded.

"He'd been on a transplant list for almost a year at that point. He'd given up all hope," she continued. "I still don't know if it was Taylor's heart he ended up getting. I know it wasn't my brother's because we got a letter one year later from the recipient of his. It was a young mother from San Francisco. She said the most wonderful things about his sacrifice and the incredible gift of life he had given her. Things that made his loss —though still devastating—a little less terrible, I guess."

Noah moved his arm over Samantha's shoulder and tugged her close.

"I always felt connected to Oliver. Like our sadness and joy were somehow linked. Like pain finally became replaced with hope," she said. "It wasn't until we met again when we were college interns that we realized who the other was. I think that history connected us in a way most people can't understand. I don't know, that probably sounds ridiculous."

"It doesn't. I firmly believe we're all linked in one way or another," Noah stated with such understanding it made her feel a little less crazy. "Most of us just never get to see how interconnected our stories really are."

Samantha smiled. "I told you he came up here as a kid, right?"

"You mentioned something about that the other night at dinner," Noah said. He looked around the room in a sweeping gaze. "This place has touched so many lives over the years. I know my Grandma has a guestbook around here somewhere. It would be interesting to take a look and see if there are any other names I recognize."

Samantha dropped her head to Noah's shoulder. "I just wanted you to know that Oliver hasn't always been this arrogant, uptight person. I knew him when he was vulnerable. When he valued the things that truly matter in life. I'm sure that man is still in there somewhere. I don't know. Sometimes, it just feels like he's not doing his best to honor the second chance he's been given."

"Then I suppose it's a good thing that life doesn't stop at second chances," Noah said.

CHAPTER 22

"*M*istletoe!" Grandma Kitty shrieked in excitement.

Joan pouted and shook her head. Her eyes scoured the room and landed on Jack near the makeshift drink station, busy at work stirring cocoa powder into the water in his Thermos with a half-eaten candy cane. Joan rushed toward him and with two hands, clutched Jack by the collar to plant a fat, smacking kiss on his bearded cheek.

"*I Saw Mommy Kissing Santa Claus!*" Samantha jumped from her chair. Her hands megaphoned her mouth as she hollered again, "*I Saw Mommy Kissing Santa Claus!*"

"Yes! You got it, darling! That's it!"

Samantha's entire team—Team Frosty, as they had ceremoniously coined themselves—erupted in a fit of celebration, high fives all around.

It was the liveliest game of Christmas charades

Noah had taken part in, and he'd had his fair share over the years. It was his grandpa's favorite game to play during this time of year. When the boys were young, Grandpa Paul would sneak in a silly clue like *Reindeer Toots* or *Moldy Fruitcake*. Without fail, either Noah or one of his brothers would draw the card and, being adolescent boys, would dissolve into a fit of immature, uproarious laughter that effectively ended the game. But it always brought a smile to the faces of each and every participant.

Noah was almost tempted to toss a childish clue into the pile tonight, if only to harken back to his grandpa's cherished memory.

Christmastime undoubtedly made Noah long for his dad and his grandpa. Holidays had a way of doing that, highlighting in your heart the loved ones who weren't near. The festivities were larger, the dinner tables longer, the absence deeper.

But tonight the room was full. Full of spirit. Full of laughter.

It didn't matter that the power had surged and then gone out an hour earlier, just as everyone expected. Nothing could dim the joy that radiated around them.

"Who's up for another round?" Noah collected the scrap pieces of paper and placed them back into the empty punch bowl.

"You just want to redeem your losing streak, brother," David snickered haughtily. "Hate to break it to you, but Team Frosty is the ultimate champion this year. Four wins to your goose egg. Hardly even a competition, if you ask me."

Noah's shoulders bobbed nonchalantly as he shrugged. "Well then, speaking of geese, how about we switch gears? Mom, you feel up to playing a little something on the piano? Perhaps *The Twelve Days of Christmas*? Six geese a-laying!"

A collective groan rumbled across the room.

"No?"

"I'm not sure I have the energy for that particular song," Audrey admitted, moving toward the piano even still. "But you know I'm always happy to play. Any other requests?"

"*Silent Night* is a favorite of mine." Joan came up next to the baby grand.

"Nothing about tonight is silent." Oliver's eyes maintained an intent watch out the closest window, and while Noah figured he referred to the weather, he also had the sense the Jensen clan was a little much for him.

"We can get kind of rowdy on family game night." Noah offered the apology like an olive branch. "All in the name of friendly competition."

Oliver's attention snapped from the window. "Oh, no. It's not the volume in here. That storm is unrelenting."

"We get one or two good ones like this each season. There will be a few downed trees. Maybe some gutters to clear out and lots and lots of plowing. But it's part of what keeps mountain living interesting.

And one thing that's reassuring is the storms always pass."

Oliver smiled weakly. "I don't mind the noise in here. I don't have any siblings, so it's actually nice to be surrounded by so many people. The voices, the laughter," Oliver disclosed to Noah. "Always figured I would have a big family of my own one day to make up for what I missed out on growing up."

Oliver's expression had been supple, melancholy even, as he regarded Samantha from across the room and spoke. But then those malleable features turned sharp at the edges. His mouth twitched, jaw ticking.

"I've messed a lot of things up in my life. Lost clients I should've hung onto. Deals that went south. I don't regret any of that. The one thing I do regret is signing my divorce papers."

Noah wasn't blind to the fact that Oliver's thumb rubbed against his empty ring finger.

"But all of this feels a little like fate. The fact that I'm back here, with her. At Christmastime."

Whether fate or just life playing itself out, Noah wasn't sure. Because it felt the same to him, but with different players. He had attributed it to fate landing Samantha on *his* property and in *his* arms. But how could he say one way or the other, really? He couldn't call it fate in one scenario and not the other, solely because it favored his feelings and situation to do so.

Was he the sort of man to stand in the way of reconciliation? He never pinned himself as that type of person. There were unspoken things that you just didn't do. Getting in the way of love fell into that category. If he was somehow a roadblock to their ultimate happiness, well, maybe he'd just have to remove himself as the barricade. But was that the right thing to do?

At one point, Samantha had loved Oliver enough to pledge her life to him before family and friends. With a vow, she'd given herself completely to him. Sickness and health, and she'd known him in both. Until death.

He had assumed, maybe even hoped, Oliver was a consummate villain. All bad and no good, which made rooting against him easy and just. But humans weren't entirely one thing or the other. And the way Samantha retold their story made Noah view the man in a different light. To paint him out to be the bad guy in all scenarios was wrong. Wasn't it?

"Do you think that's what she wants?" Noah summoned the courage to ask the question that clawed inside him. "To try things again?"

"We have history. We have shared goals. We have a business." Oliver's voice was burdened with regret, like a man who had gambled it all, only to come up mournfully empty. "Samantha isn't the type of person to give up on a good thing. And that's the problem. Our marriage—it wasn't good at the end. Both of us could see that. But maybe that shouldn't've been our *end*. If we rode out the storm, so to speak, then we could have come out on the other side even stronger,"

Oliver elaborated. "I think I owe you for that clarity, Noah."

"Owe me?"

"Well, owe Cedar Crest, at the very least. This place has a way of highlighting the things that matter." Oliver's palm met the middle of Noah's back, right between his shoulder blades. "Maybe I even have this storm to thank. Like you said, they always pass."

THE CANDLES HAD TURNED INTO WAXY POOLS BY the time the lights powered on around daybreak. Between the fire and the generous supply of pillar candles Grandma Kitty kept on hand for times such as these, they hardly noticed the lack of power. All their needs were met, be that warmth, light, or even entertainment.

It had been a long time since their family was together in full, and the additional company of the Days—and Oliver, too—made time pass swiftly and sweetly. New memories were created, friendships formed.

Noah had pulled up a chair and sat near the hearth to stoke the fire now and then with the poker, pretending his focus was necessary there to keep the flames churning and the place heated. It wasn't, and the fire would blaze on just fine without his assistance. But he required a job that allowed him to stay on the periphery. He had no room for anything else in his head, no place for focus or concentration.

He was falling for Samantha and he had a hunch she was doing the same. But they weren't completely in love. Not yet, at least.

They'd shared a kiss and a handful of experiences he would treasure.

But Oliver and Samantha shared a marriage. A house and a last name. Their level of connection was beyond anything beginning between Noah and Samantha. While Noah had assumed things with Oliver had already ended, maybe this was their middle. Maybe it was just a pause.

Once the power had returned, they all agreed it best to take advantage of their second winds (or maybe third or fourth, at that point) and do the hard work of clearing the doorways and paths of dumped snow before stealing away for some much needed shuteye.

The plow made quick work of most of it, and so did the team of shovelers who gladly helped get the property where it needed to be. Never had Noah been so grateful for the cheerful smiles and hearty effort. It was as though a night full of games and carols was enough to sustain them, giving them the energy to crank out the tasks in record time.

Even Oliver, decked in his fine apparel and expensive shoes, pitched in.

Noah had dropped into bed around eight in the morning, exhausted and spent in both body and mind. It wasn't until noon when Noah finally arose, and while four hours of sleep was half his typical amount, it would have to do.

The production team showed up shortly after lunch. They had had to wait for highway lanes to be cleared and the resulting traffic to subside, so it didn't matter that the Jensens were also getting a late start. They were all at the mercy of the mountain, it seemed.

By the time Noah was showered and ready to face the day, he had three voicemails waiting for him on his cell phone. Two repair inquiries and one message from Father Christmas, graciously bowing out of the running, not that there was much of one anymore. He had been offered the role of Santa Claus at the Victorian Christmas in Nevada City, a fitting opportunity he couldn't pass up. Noah called him back to thank him for his flexibility throughout their chaotic week and then dialed Samantha.

"If the whole thing hasn't completely turned your parents off, let them know they're the only Mr. and Mrs. Claus left," he said. "And that's if there's even a part for them in the new commercial. I'm not sure what you and Marty have planned."

"I'll let them know," she answered. "And they will still have a role—a small but important one. Like the star at the top of a tree."

He could hear the smile in her voice, and then a pause.

"Will I get to see you today?" she asked.

"I need to head into town for a few jobs this afternoon, but I'll be back before dinner. Plus, I figure it'll be best for me to stay out of everyone's hair while the team is shooting. I know your time with them is limited."

"It is, but believe it or not, I think we've got a really good vision for everything. The director is totally on board with my ideas and has a lot of her own, too. I think you'll be pleasantly surprised with the final piece."

Anything would be better than what they currently had, which was next to nothing. In fairness, they had a simple website where bookings could be made directly through the page, but that was the extent of their advertising efforts. Unless you had visited Cedar Crest before, there was little reason to even know it still existed. In a way, it almost felt like it didn't.

"I'm sure I will love it," he said. "I'll check in once I've wrapped up my day. And Samantha?"

"Yes?"

"Thank you," Noah said. His throat scratched as he swallowed. "You have gone above and beyond in every way imaginable. More than expected and certainly more than necessary. And I can't thank you enough for that."

"That's what friends are for," she answered cheerily before they said their goodbyes.

Friends. The word taunted him like a schoolyard bully. It could've been a slip of the tongue, or it could've even been the honest to goodness truth. Because friendship was the foundation of any meaningful relationship. Noah believed that. But he sensed a limiting quality in her tone, like her words were meant to be informative, too. They were friends. *Just* friends.

Had Oliver said something to her about his intentions the night before? About his plan to fight for her and win her back? There was certainly the opportunity for him to bring it up, what with the countless hours of nothing to do other than commune and carol. Noah had noticed them in conversation here and there, but nothing that looked intense.

Noah made the drive into town, reprimanding those mounting insecurities as he spun the dial on the Jeep's stereo. Every station played a steady stream of Christmas songs, one after the other, like the countdown of connected paper rings. The inherently merry vocals suffused Noah with joy. He really did love this season. From the snowcapped mountains to a cup of spiced cider to the generosity of a stranger, every bit of the holiday meant something to him.

He would focus on that because it was the only good thing to do.

His first job went quickly: cutting up a spruce that had fallen uncomfortably close to the Fredrickson's house. As his chainsaw roared to life, Noah hummed along with it. It was honest work and he was thankful for the chance to help his friends and neighbors.

Todd Fredrickson—the family's eldest boy, home

on winter break from UCLA—took the discarded pieces and split them into firewood to be piled against the shed for future use. They labored in assembly-line fashion until the once grand tree was stacked and stored.

Even though the evergreen met its end naturally, it was still useful, still necessary. Nothing wasted. Noah liked that.

He swung by *The Guzzler* for a quick cup of joe, then circled back to order two more. Thomas Ridley had an electric stove that wouldn't start, and Noah never liked to show up at their house empty-handed. When she was healthy enough to do so, Bessie would make a loaf of banana chocolate chip bread or have a tin of frosted sugar cookies ready for Noah to take with him. Even as frail as she was, she would consistently give him a hard time, saying he could stand to gain a pound or two. And her butter-soaked, baked goods ensured that was likely to happen.

"How is she?" Noah whispered upon entering the small mountain home. He handed off the two cups of coffee and gave Thomas a thoughtful look.

Noah took Thomas's matching low volume to mean Bessie was resting, much like usual. "Failing, I hate to say." Thomas placed the coffee on the kitchen counter and grasped Noah's shoulder with his hand.

"Any word from the doctor?"

"None. But I don't believe we need his diagnosis to confirm what our hearts already know," the man said. "Our time together is on its last downhill run, I gather. But golly, it's been a good life. A real good one." Thomas's fingers closed around Noah's shoulder and squeezed before releasing. "She's not eating much these days, but this morning she woke up with a hankering for Shepherd's Pie. Got it all ready the best I could with the ingredients we had on hand, and when I went to preheat the oven, nothing."

"Have you checked the breaker?"

"I haven't. With all the snow, I wasn't sure I'd be able to make it out to the panel. This knee of mine acts up with the storms. I hate to call you down here just for something as simple as that—"

"It's no trouble at all, Thomas. I've got warm clothes and some cold weather boots, so I'm well prepared for a little trek in the snow."

"I know Bessie usually has something made up for you to take back to the cabins to share with your family. I'm sad to say she hasn't felt up to spending much time in the kitchen as of late. But if you can get the stove up and running and you're not short on time, you can stay until the pie's done and take a slice for the road."

"That's very thoughtful, but I'm hoping to get back to the cabins in time for dinner."

"Someone waiting for you there?"

"Is it that obvious?" Noah chuckled and scratched at his neck. "Yes, actually. There is someone."

"The young gal from the hardware store?"

Noah thought back to the day Samantha had joined him on his errands. "The very one."

"She's a beauty. That long, blonde hair. A lot like my Bessie's, back in the day. Believe it or not, we haven't always been old timers. Back in our prime, we were really lookers." The man laughed so forcefully it nearly sent him into a coughing fit. After he rallied, he wiped his eye. "Glad to see you've found your girl, Noah. You deserve a good one."

"I'm not entirely sure she's mine."

"Oh, I wouldn't doubt yourself so. My guess is someday you'll be looking back at the end of your run with her by your side. I have a good mind when it comes to these things."

"I'm not even sure we're on the chairlift together, let alone the run."

"Well then, that's entirely your own fault, because the way she looked at you in the hardware store said she was ready to take the leap." Thomas's gaze swung down the hall, toward the room where his beloved bride rested. "And if I can give you some advice, don't waste even one minute. When all is said and done, there just aren't any minutes to spare."

CHAPTER 23

*S*amantha stayed under the steaming cascade of hot water until her shriveled fingers warned her it was well past time to get out. She didn't want to turn into a complete prune, but the water felt so good against her aching muscles and weary joints.

She wished there was a way to rinse the mind of troubles the same way a long shower refreshed the body.

It wasn't unreasonable to say it had been the longest day of her life. Some of that could be attributed to the fact that yesterday bled into today without the buffer of sleep to split the days in two. When was the last time she'd pulled an all-nighter like that? It had to be in college, and even then, she wasn't sure she'd put as much effort into her studies as she had into the Cedar Crest Cabins commercial.

She was well aware her job as a talent agent mostly began and ended with getting her parents the original audition. But over the course of a few days, her investment in this place took deeper root and her involvement followed in line. Occasionally, she worried she was possibly overstepping. But her heart told her that wasn't the case, as she knew the Jensens had few other options.

This Christmas marketing campaign was a last-ditch effort. There was no sense in giving anything other than one-hundred percent. And that's exactly what everyone had done today.

Even with the rush placed on production, it would be a couple of days before they would have any footage or preliminary edits to view. That was fine. Of course, Samantha was eager to see if it had all worked out in the end. If her vision translated well on screen. But a day of mental rest truly sounded like heaven.

And it didn't hurt that Cedar Crest was just that—heavenly. Snow dressed the mountain in immaculate white. Tree branches bent downward, laden with the burdening weight of fresh snow. Earlier, Samantha even glimpsed a family of deer out of her back cabin window. A doe with her fawn. Their spindly legs sank into the snow and left little tracks in their wake as they eased in and out of the meandering forest typography.

It was as though Samantha was in the very middle of a Christmas postcard or holiday-inspired painting. She wished she could capture her surroundings in either of those forms. Before leaving for home, she'd have to make time to take her own photographs of the property. It was a sight she would never want to forget.

Once Samantha emerged from her shower, she quickly blow-dried her hair and pulled on a pair of olive green leggings, selecting her over-sized, slouchy black sweater from her luggage to complete the comfortable outfit. The Jensen women were planning to meet for cider and knitting in the small sitting area where guests checked in. Though Samantha had only picked up yarn and knitting needles a handful of times in her life, Kitty assured her it wasn't as difficult as it seemed.

She slipped on her jacket and headed toward the building up the hill.

Samantha remembered the cozy space fondly, but not just for its décor or ambiance. It was where she'd first glimpsed Noah, standing tall and somewhat flustered behind the desk, looking out of place and yet still at home all at once. He'd been endearing from the very start. She could scarcely believe that was only days ago. So much had happened, both in their timeline and within her heart.

As she slipped her hands into her coat pockets and continued her walk, she reflected back on her limited experiences with love. Had her connection with Oliver been the same—that swift and strong? Of course she remembered the giddy, overflowing sensation of young love. Maybe it was only infatuation the first time they'd met at the hospital as teenagers. But several years later, when they were in their early twenties, their relationship matured, gradually and then on a more meaningful level.

If she remembered correctly, it did take some time to be certain her connection with Oliver had more to do with real, lasting affection and less to do with shared work interests and skills. In the end, she'd lumped it all together, figuring those occupational commonalities, along with attraction and friendship, were the building blocks of a successful relationship.

She still couldn't understand how she'd gotten it so wrong.

But Oliver seemed different lately. Maybe it was the altitude getting to him. She chuckled at the thought, but couldn't dismiss the tender way he'd looked at her throughout the day. The way he talked with her parents like a son would and not as an estranged ex-relative. It called back to a time her heart had almost completely forgotten.

Just yesterday, she'd shared with Noah about the man Oliver had once been. How she wished he'd take seriously the treasured second chance at life he'd been given. She hadn't made it on a star or to the man in red, but she couldn't help but feel that wish had been miraculously granted.

And if it had, what was she to do with that?

Samantha removed her hand from her pocket and slipped it onto the door handle, grateful for the distraction of good new friends and a warm drink. These were thoughts she would have to tuck away for later.

"You made it!" Vera exclaimed in her customarily boisterous voice. "I would get up to hug you, but I'm afraid I'm pretty wedged into this chair at the moment."

Samantha shook her head. "Don't get up on my account. You look perfectly cozy. Stay put."

"Looks can be deceiving. Comfort is a thing I haven't experienced in months. This little gal is running out of room in here." She patted her stomach with affection. "Eviction day is coming soon; I can feel it."

"Come on over and sit next to me, Samantha." Grandma Kitty indicated the empty cushion next to her on the couch. "Saved you a spot."

Audrey sat in a rocker closest to the crackling fire, at work on what Samantha figured to be a baby blanket for her future granddaughter. Soft pink, fuzzy yarn coiled in and out of row upon row. Just like at the piano, Audrey's fingers were dexterous and delicate, bringing into being something from nothing. These Jensens—they were a skilled sort of people… and caring, thoughtful, and generous to boot.

The list could go on and on. And it did. As the minutes ticked by in the presence of these precious women, Samantha noted all the things she cherished about this family. Ultimately, it was the fact that they made those around them instantly *feel* like family that set them apart. They weren't too hurried to invest in others. Not too rushed to take note of the people around them.

They were hospitable, and these cabins couldn't be managed by a more fitting group.

Samantha didn't even attempt to learn how to knit. She was perfectly happy to sit with a pile of wound-up string in her lap, a mug of cider nestled between her palms. The warming spices met her tongue as she took an unhurried sip. Nutmeg. Clove. Even a little ground ginger, if her taste buds were correct.

Grandma Kitty bumped Samantha's shoulder and clicked her tongue. "I used maple syrup for sweetener," she said with a grin. "I know you're a fan."

"It's delicious," Samantha affirmed.

"You want to make something?" Kitty's gaze bounced down to Samantha's lap of tangled yarn. "I'd be happy to teach you an easy garter stitch."

"Oh, that's okay. But thank you. I'm happy just to be here with you ladies. The fire is lovely and the cider is delicious. I don't want to ruin any of that with failed attempts at knitting."

"You'd be a fast learner; I'm certain of it." Kitty patted Samantha's leg. "But you also deserve some downtime, too. So if you're content just relaxing, then that makes me happy. You've put in more than your fair share of work around here. While we can't really pay you much monetarily speaking, I was thinking I could at least give you a new skill as some form of payment. But if knitting isn't your thing, then that's no problem at all."

"You've given me so much more than I think you

realize, Kitty." Samantha took a deep breath. Tendrils of steam from the cider tickled her nose. She felt as though she teetered on the edge of tears. "You know, I've always been so focused on discovering the talents in others, I've never really taken the time to figure out what I'm good at."

Grandma Kitty lowered her knitting needles to her lap, lending her full attention.

"We'll see how it all sorts out in the end, but I'm proud about the work we did here today," Samantha admitted. "Usually, I just find the right people for the right auditions and don't get to see things to fruition. It's exciting to be part of the process, especially when it's for such a worthy cause."

"I'm glad to hear it." Kitty beamed. "So very glad to hear it."

CHAPTER 24

*D*inner earlier that night had arguably been Grandma Kitty's best menu yet: slow-roasted prime rib with all the comfort food fixings. Crispy red potatoes drenched in olive oil and strewn with fresh parsley and Italian seasonings. French green beans just the way Noah liked them—sautéed with enough butter that they no longer even tasted like vegetables.

Kitty had said it was a trial run for their Christmas dinner and that she wanted to share this meal with those who wouldn't be there when the holiday rolled around.

Noah wouldn't let his mind linger on that fact—that Samantha and Joan and Jack would head out in just a couple of days. He pushed that aside and valued the moment for what it was. As he always said, there was no use letting tomorrow's worries occupy today's thoughts.

At first, no one really noticed when Audrey snuck away after the meal. They'd been immersed in a lively debate as to whether the original eight reindeer were relatives or just happened to be gathered from the same reindeer herd. Someone even suggested they were rescues Santa had chosen from a North Pole reindeer shelter. It was silly, and the steady stream of spiked eggnog might've added to the volume and intensity in which they debated.

But when Audrey had emerged from the kitchen, a glowing array of candles sunk into the top layer of an iced chocolate cake, the room fell to a hush.

"Happy birthday to you," Audrey started in her sweet soprano voice. "Happy birthday to you."

One by one, the others joined in.

"Happy birthday, dear *Samantha*," they belted. "Happy birthday to you!"

Her eyes sprung open wide. "But it's not my birthday. Not for another few weeks."

"It's your birthday *month* and that's how we like to celebrate around here," Audrey had said. She'd placed the cake in front of Samantha and nudged toward it. "Go ahead. Make a wish."

Noah met Samantha's gaze for the briefest of moments before her eyes fell shut as she made the silent wish. It was a flicker of connection between them, but enough for him to heap all of his hopes upon that very wish. He could only pray it was the same wish he'd held in his heart.

After dinner, they had parted ways. The women

had mentioned something about a knitting circle and cider, and while he wanted more than anything to spend additional time with Samantha, he would leave her to that activity. He was good at a lot of things, but having the patience to loop rows of yarn together wasn't in his wheelhouse.

Instead, he found himself alone in the woodshop again.

Samantha wouldn't be at Cedar Crest for her birthday, but that didn't change the fact that Noah wanted to make her something. A gift that helped convey his feelings where his words ultimately failed.

He took a block from the stack and began to carve.

Over the last couple of days, he'd practiced the motions, learning how much pressure to apply with the knife to shave away small portions of wood. A camping lantern illuminated his workspace in a funnel of amber light, and snow fell just outside the only window in airy flakes that stuck to the glass every now and then. The place was serene, which allowed Noah to focus on his project as he honed his chiseling skills.

At least an hour had passed when he saw a blur cross through his line of sight just on the other side of the window. A bear was his first thought, but that didn't seem plausible. They only had one resident black bear the locals dubbed Big Cody, and he knew for a fact that particular animal had gone into hibernation a few weeks earlier. Apparently, Charlie Haskins, the owner of the nearby snowmobile rental company, saw Big Cody retreat to his den on their hillside property for the winter, giving the man one final gruff grunt before squeezing into his snowy cavern.

With that worry tucked out of the way, Noah wondered if the shadow had been a mere figment of his imagination. His mind did have a way of running away with itself. But when the woodshop door began to rattle like someone—or something—was attempting to force it open, he listened to his gut, knowing it rarely steered him wrong. He grabbed the longer of the two knives he'd used for carving and wrapped his fingers securely around the handle.

The door jostled again and something close to a growl reverberated through the wood partition.

Lifting the carving implement over his shoulder like he would a baseball bat or even a golf club, he eased across the shed, his footsteps purposefully light, breaths quickening.

"Hey, bear!" he announced loudly. He'd learned the greeting on a survival show he had watched years ago where contestants were left out in the great, wild outdoors with not much more than the shirts on their backs. "Hey, bear." His voice quivered more audibly this time.

The door flew open.

"What is wrong with you?" Marty stood on the other side of the threshold. "Put that knife down. You're going to hurt someone."

"Why not just knock?" Tossing the tool to the

workbench, Noah drug a hand over his brow and sighed his relief. "You almost gave me a heart attack."

"Is there a reason I would need to knock? Last I checked, you don't own this woodshop."

"No, but I'm obviously in here."

"I can see that." Marty stepped into the place and shut the door behind him. "And now I'm in here, too."

Noah knew he wouldn't get anywhere with this. He tossed his hands up and waved him off. "Okay, fine. What is it that you're doing in here, anyway?"

"I'm here to carve."

He didn't want his surprise to register on his face, but he had little control over the shock that likely manipulated his features. "You woodwork?"

"A little. But I'm working on something that's sort of time sensitive, so I'll need you to clear out so I can have the space."

"Well, I'm doing the same. Working on something time sensitive." He hated that he always felt like such a younger brother when he interacted with Marty, even though they were both grown adults. "Looks like we'll have to learn to share."

The growl that rumbled Marty's chest mimicked his earlier one. "The thing I'm working on is private."

"So is mine."

Marty rolled his eyes. "You are annoying; you know that? I really don't know what Samantha sees in you."

"Has she said something to you?" An instant lump

formed in Noah's throat. "About me?"

All at once, Noah was as insecure as a teenager passing a *check YES or NO* note to his crush.

"It's obvious she likes you," Marty huffed. "Are you that dense?"

Talking with Marty about his feelings for Samantha wasn't wise. Noah knew that full well.

"Never mind. Listen, I'm going to work on my project over here." Noah made a sweeping, circular motion over his workspace with his hand. "And you can work over there. I won't bother you. Promise."

"You already are."

Noah groaned. "What is your deal, Marty? Have I done something to upset you?"

Marty just made his way to his designated work area, ignoring Noah's question like he had earplugs jammed deep into his ear canals.

"Marty."

"What?" His brother whirled around.

"What's going on?"

"Nothing's going on. Now, will you please just let me work in peace?"

"I don't like this." Noah's hand passed through the space between them. "I don't like this tension. It's been here since we were kids."

"I was hardly around long enough back then for you to have any memory of it."

"I have memories, Marty."

"Yeah? Memories of the three years I spent in juvie? Or the time I crashed Dad's snowmobile and then framed that Nicholson kid for it? Or maybe when I flunked out of high school? Because I have *those* memories, Noah. Those are the memories I have. Not of Christmases here at Cedar Crest. Not of traditions and meals around the table and family and holidays."

"You weren't gone for all of it."

"No, but I was gone for the times that mattered."

Noah felt cold, both in his heart toward his brother and in the icy shed where they stood across the room from one another like a standoff.

"You know, I want to feel sorry for you, but that was all your doing. You're the one who made the choices that led to you being away for those things. And honestly, even when you were here, you were never really *here*."

"You think I don't know that?"

"I honestly don't know what to think, Marty! You never tell me what you're thinking, so how am I supposed to know?"

"Fine, then. This is what I'm thinking." Marty's hands curled around the ledge of the workbench separating them, his broad frame looming over the table in a stance that looked like a grizzly about to lunge. "I'm thinking I've wasted all of my good years making stupid decisions that have gotten me nowhere. *That's* what I'm thinking."

"You've got plenty of years left, Marty. Jeez, you're not even thirty-six. You arguably have a whole life ahead of you."

"I'm talking about all of my years *here*. At the cabins. On this mountain." Marty pushed back from the table. "What if we can't save the place, Noah?" His voice cracked, just a hint of vulnerability slipping through his force field of armor. "What if this is it for Grandpa and Dad's legacy?"

"*We* are Grandpa and Dad's legacy." Noah tried to marshal control over his volume. He wasn't about to get into a shouting match with his brother. That wouldn't get them anywhere. "Don't you understand that?" Noah implored. "It's not about the physical place, it's about you and me and David. We're the legacy. We carry their tradition of family wherever we go, whether it's on this mountain or halfway across the world."

Marty's jaw remained clenched, his shoulders squared, but the hardness in his gaze softened enough for Noah to notice.

"I know we haven't always seen eye to eye, but you're my brother, Marty. Always will be. Believe it or not, I care about you. We're family," Noah said. "Regardless of the things that have happened in our past, I will always want you to be a part of my future."

Marty shook out his shoulders. "Ugh. Enough with all the mushy talk." He flopped onto a stool and picked up a chisel. "I've got a project I need to finish up." He kept his eyes down, focused on his hands and the tool when he added, "But I care about you, too, brother. I just have a really stupid way of showing it."

CHAPTER 25

*T*he text hadn't revealed much, other than to meet outside the cabins in a half hour and to dress warmly. That wasn't a problem, as the majority of the clothes Samantha had brought with her were meant for mountain weather.

She'd already re-worn a few items during her stay, but by layering or adding a cute scarf or beanie, she didn't feel as though she was repeating the same outfit. And just last night, Vera had gifted her with the most beautiful cranberry-colored knit wrap she'd been working on by the fire. An early birthday present, she'd said. It was gorgeous, and Samantha couldn't wait to try it on.

A full night's sleep had also done wonders for her mood and energy. Last night, while enjoying the company of the Jensen women in the sitting area, she had nodded off on multiple occasions. It wasn't until she felt Kitty drape a blanket across her as she rested her head and shut her eyes that Samantha knew she needed to excuse herself to head to a proper bed. The others surely didn't need the soundtrack of her snoring while they knitted and chatted by the hearth.

She'd slept fast and hard. That was until her phone trilled across the nightstand in the morning. At first, the buzzing of the incoming text message that roused Samantha disgruntled her, but a quick glance toward the bedside clock read it was nearing ten. That was definitely considered sleeping in, even for her. And while the heavy quilt and warmth trapped beneath it beckoned her to stay, her interest had been piqued.

Noah had something planned, and she couldn't wait to find out what that might be. She rushed to get ready and made her way outside.

Vera lifted her voice across the snowy courtyard when she caught sight of Samantha. "Hurry up! It's Snowman Saturday!"

"What is Snowman Saturday?"

"Just another Cedar Crest tradition. And we have Marty to thank for resurrecting it," Noah said. He gifted Samantha a smile that made her entire body warm even more than the wool blankets had. She knew her cheeks likely reddened with a flush. That dimpled grin had its way of melting her completely.

"Can it still be called a tradition if we haven't done it in years?" David brushed his gloves together to knock off bits of collected snow. "Is there some rule about that?"

"Tradition is anything passed down through the generations. There's no rule about how often you have to do it. Just that you carry it on," Marty stated. He gave Noah just a sliver of a smile, but Samantha glimpsed the brotherly exchange. "And that's what we're doing today—carrying it on."

Samantha's parents were there too, along with Oliver, who stood a few feet off. His head was bowed, his thumb scrolling over his phone. When he lifted his eyes to meet Samantha's, the edges crinkled into a smile and he held her gaze with an intensity that almost startled her. "Morning."

"Morning," Samantha returned. She broke eye contact. "I'm assuming Snowman Saturday has something to do with building snowmen?"

"Shoot. How d'you figure that out?" Noah teased.

"Oh, you know. My sleuthing skills are off the charts."

Noah flashed a smirk and continued, "We'll divide into teams. Then we'll each have five minutes to gather whatever items you'll need for a proper snowman. You can raid the kitchen, rummage through your cabin—anything you want—but when that timer is up, it's go time."

"This is a competition," Marty clarified. "So you'll want to get creative."

"How is the winner decided?" Samantha inquired, zipping her jacket all the way up to her chin.

"We'll all vote. Of course, you won't be able to

vote for your own. The winner gets bragging rights. It's about all we can afford," Noah joked.

"And the team with the least votes has to make dinner!" Grandma Kitty added gleefully.

"That's not part of the tradition," David said.

"Well, considering I'm the oldest Jensen and it was my dear husband who started Snowman Saturday, I think I can fudge the rules as I see fit," she said. She placed her hands on her hips. "And this old lady could use a break from cooking for a night."

"Nobody's going to argue with you there, Grandma. You deserve a night off," Noah smiled, then raised his wrist to eye level. "On your mark, get set—"

"Wait!" Vera butted in. "We need to divide into teams."

"Ah, yes." He nodded. "I knew I was forgetting something. What's the best way to do that?"

"There are nine of us. I'm fine working on my own, so just number off one through four and you'll have your remaining pairs," Marty suggested flatly.

It wasn't a bad idea. Easy and simple. But based on their positions in the small circle, Samantha knew it meant she wouldn't be partnered with Noah. Her heart sank a little with that.

"Okay, I'll start. One," Noah began.

"Two," Samantha said next. And so on and so forth until they were all numbered off.

She didn't mean to, but when Oliver also recited

the word *'two,'* she winced. Of the members in the group, he was the last partner she hoped to draw.

She knew she already worked well with Marty from their time at the piano. Vera would be a delight with her bubbly personality and crafty ideas. Grandma Kitty was always good company, as were Audrey and David. And either of her parents would be a joy to be partnered with. Like old times.

And Noah—how fun would it be to build a snowman with him? She could envision the activity already, the way he would undoubtedly turn it into an impromptu, all-in-fun snowball fight or how they'd end up on their backs, creating snow angels in the fresh powder, arms and legs fanned out and swishing in big, sweeping motions.

But Oliver? She worked with him day in and day out. Their final snowman would be a masterpiece, of that she had no doubt, but his company wasn't what she desired for the afternoon.

Somehow, judging by the hopeful look crossing his features, he didn't share that same disappointment.

"Hey, partner." He came up to her side as the duos paired off. "This is sort of kismet, no?"

"It's something." Samantha's lips pressed to a flat line. Despite her frustration, she wasn't one to shy away from competition. If she had to be Oliver's partner, she would make the best of it, and that meant building the best snowman. She began to brainstorm. "Did you bring your tweed cap? The one you got on our trip to England right out of college?"

"I did."

"Good. When we break to gather items, be sure to grab that. It screams snowman hat. And I'll gather a few things I have on hand. I've got a set of false lashes I can donate to the cause, along with a scarf that'll be perfect to wrap around his neck."

"Got it."

Just then, Noah coughed to gather the attention of the pairs buzzing in discussion as they planned out their snowman strategies.

"Everyone ready this time?" he asked, looking around the circle for confirmation. "On your mark, get set...*GO!*"

The teams set out like runners at the starting line, bumbling across the snow toward their cabins, the dining hall, and the check-in lodge. Samantha even saw Noah and her mom move toward the woodshed, likely hoping to find some treasure within the old workshop.

She split from Oliver and amassed all she could find within her cabin for the competition: a pair of argyle print mittens, a few items from her toiletry bag, a set of small, bauble ornaments for the eyes and a decorative pine cone for a possible nose.

At some point in time, Noah had gotten his hands on a blow horn, and at the five-minute mark, he blasted the alarm. All teams rushed back, out of breath and weighed down with armloads of supplies.

"Looks like we'll have the best dressed snowmen this

side of Cedar Crest," Noah said as he glanced around, looking pleased at the sight. "So here are the details. Each team will have one hour. You can assemble your snowman wherever you like. Just keep it within a reasonable walking distance from the cabins so we don't have to traipse all over when it comes time to vote. When time's up, I'll sound the horn again and we'll reassemble back here. You'll have just under a minute to get back from the moment the horn goes off. If you're late, your team will be immediately disqualified."

"And if you don't finish building your snowman within the timeframe allotted, you'll be disqualified," David added.

"And if you don't use three round sections to build your snowman, you'll also be disqualified," Grandma Kitty went on. "Plus, you'll need some sort of hat, eyes, nose, mouth, and arms. Standard snowman parts."

"Seems like you guys are pretty fond of rules and disqualifications," Samantha joked.

"One year, Dad and Grandpa won solely through the process of elimination," Noah said. "The issue was, they didn't really make up the thing about disqualifications until after the contest was over and they started rejecting our snowmen left and right. Mine didn't meet the minimum height requirement. Didn't know there was one. Marty's circles weren't round enough. Didn't know they had to be. I think Dad even cut Mom from the competition because her snowman started to melt before we even had the chance to vote on a winner."

Audrey nodded in agreement, a reflective look crossing her face.

Noah carried on, "At least I'm being fair and filling you in on the rules of the game before it starts."

David elbowed his brother. "But you're forgetting the number one rule."

"Oh yeah? What's that?"

"To have fun!" he shouted. "Come on now, let's get this competition underway!"

Less hurried than earlier, the groups separated. Oliver was slow to move, so Samantha took the lead.

"Let's construct ours behind my cabin. There's a little spot I can see from my window and it'll be the ideal backdrop for our snowman. It's picturesque and scenic, full of woodland charm. A fitting spot for a winter snowman."

"I'm on board with that."

He had taken the items from Samantha's hands. Though she appreciated the help, the act of chivalry was foreign coming from Oliver.

"Remember that time we built a snowman on our trip to Park City?" Oliver asked, following in her boot tracks like a puppy. "I think it was our third Christmas together. We stayed in that chateau that had the snow-park right outside the door. You would watch all the kids from the breakfast nook window every morning and you kept asking if I thought we were too old to make a snowman of our own. Said you hadn't built one since childhood." He kept his eyes trained forward on her as they walked toward the edge of her cabin. His gaze was intense and full of something Samantha couldn't pinpoint. She diverted her focus toward the path ahead of them and shrugged off the mounting discomfort. "As I remember correctly, ours wasn't the most well-constructed snowman. Didn't last all that long once we built him."

"He sure didn't. Got plowed into by that rogue downhill skier and lost two-thirds of his body. It was more than a little disturbing. Snowman pieces everywhere." Samantha snorted, trying to stifle her laugh under her gloved palm. "And his head rolled all the way down to the ice rink at the base of the hill. Remember that?" At this point, she couldn't keep in her laughter and it sputtered out noisily. "Came to a rest right next to that sweet, young family. I still feel like we gave that poor little girl a year's worth of nightmares."

"I don't know, her older brother seemed to think it was pretty hysterical."

"He picked it up and threw it at her!"

"What any big brother would do. It turned into an epic snowball fight. Everyone got in on it. Even us." Oliver placed their items to the ground when Samantha came to a stop, then paused before saying, "The Jensens are a pretty great family, aren't they?"

Samantha bristled. The unexpected shift in conversation caught her completely off guard. "What makes you say that?"

"I don't know. It's just—something about that particular memory—it seems like it could happen at a place like this. Heck, I can even picture Noah and his brothers as the ones tossing around the snowballs."

"Don't forget Grandma Kitty. She'd be in on it, too," Samantha said. "But yes, they are pretty great." She crouched down to the snow and began to mound a few handfuls of loose powder for the base.

"It's what I wanted for us, you know."

"Wanted what?"

"A big family. Lots of kids. Brothers and sisters. I wanted that."

She didn't look up, but shifted along the ground to drag more snow into her pile. They were on the clock, after all. They'd have to talk while they worked, though she couldn't say this conversation was one she really wished to continue.

"As I recall, you wanted to be the number one talent agency in Northern California."

"Sure, I wanted that, too. But my dreams weren't mutually exclusive."

"Maybe not for you. But for me, your dreams were."

Oliver's brow lifted like a question mark at the end of a sentence.

"How do you think we got to the top?" Samantha asked rhetorically when he looked at her in muddled confusion. "It was a partnership, Oliver. You couldn't have done it without me. But all this talk of a big family that you're just *now* mentioning—that would have been at the sacrifice of our business. I'm just not sure that's something you were willing to give up at the time."

"It wouldn't've necessarily had to be that way. We could've gotten a nanny. Had my mom or dad or your parents help out. We could've made it work. Have a large family while also running a large agency."

Samantha packed the snow under her palm, clamping it down as she huffed with the motions. "You say you want this—what the Jensens have. A tightknit, big ol' family. How would that even have been an option for us?"

"We could've had a daycare at the agency. Lots of businesses do that. Then we could've been around to give our kids the attention they needed, when they needed it."

"Oliver, you couldn't even give me the attention I needed!" Her hands came down firmly onto the icy ground in a smack. She popped to her feet.

Oliver looked instantly crestfallen. "Samantha."

"I'm serious. Do you know why we never had children? Or even really discussed starting a family?"

Again, his features—devoid of any understanding —remained blank.

"Because you and I never felt like a family, Oliver." She pulled in a measured breath through her nostrils and tilted her face heavenward, willing her voice to conceal the emotion that coursed through her entire being. "Creating a family is more than just adding a child."

Oliver came up to her. "I know that, Samantha." He took her hands into his. "Of course, I know that."

"But do you?" She pulled from his grasp and stepped back, needing some physical distance between them. "We couldn't even create a sense of family when it was just the two of us."

"We were a family, Sam. We did all the things families do. We ate meals together every day."

"I would bring you a croissant I picked up from the coffee shop and toss it onto your desk on my way into my office. That's hardly sharing a meal."

"We went on vacations together. We spent time with our parents each week. We shared a house."

"But what about sharing our hopes for our future? We had a business plan for Knight and Day, but we had no plan for us. No goals, no dreams. For goodness' sake, this is the first I'm hearing of your desire to have a big family."

"Because I never realized that was what I wanted until now." He narrowed the gap and took her by the shoulders, his deep blue eyes fastened on hers in a gaze that felt all too familiar. "You said it wasn't a sacrifice I would've been able to make when we were starting out with the agency, and maybe you're right about that. Maybe I wouldn't have then. But I want to now. I'm willing to give all of that up if it means we could try to make this work."

"This?" Her shoulders stiffened. "There is no 'this'."

"You can't tell me there's not still something here."

His grip felt less possessive on her and suddenly turned affectionate in the way his hands brushed against her shoulders like a caress. She wanted to shrug him off, to shrug off the physical contact and toss away the words he spoke. Words she had prayed he would say years ago when the thread of the marriage was unraveling like a spool rolling across the floor.

Words she would have given anything to hear back then.

Words that could have saved their marriage.

"Oliver, a part of me will always love you. You know that. We share too much history for me not to feel that for you. But we weren't good together."

"And I take full credit for that."

"You shouldn't. It wasn't all your fault. I'm to blame, too. I held you to expectations that I never shared with you and that wasn't fair."

"Then tell me what you expect from me now and I'll be that," Oliver said. "I'll be whatever you need."

"I don't want you to change for me, Oliver."

"I'm not changing for you; I'm changing because of you." He inclined his head a few inches to where she could feel his breath against her cheeks. "Losing you changed me. And maybe that's what needed to happen. Don't they always say, 'you never know a good thing until it's gone?'"

Stinging tears pricked the backs of her eyes and

Samantha squeezed them shut to ward off the impending freefall.

"That's just it, Oliver. I don't want to be with someone who realizes my worth when I'm no longer theirs. I want to be with someone who values what they have, when they have it," she said. "And I feel so blessed that life has recently gifted me another opportunity to discover that."

CHAPTER 26

Snowman Saturday was loads of fun. And to see Marty take the helm was the sweetest part of it all. He hadn't suddenly righted all of his wrongs or slipped into the role of the family patriarch, but it was the most apparent attempt at reconciliation he'd ever made and that was a blessing.

In the end, only four snowmen were ultimately eligible. Oliver and Samantha never fully constructed one, and when the group came around to view what they assumed would be the team's entry, Samantha smiled sheepishly and asked what they all felt like for dinner.

Noah would not hold her to it, but she insisted, saying it was the least they could do. Rules were rules. But neither Samantha nor Oliver considered themselves chefs by any means. Instead, they opted to treat the Jensen's—along with Jack and Joan—to a formal dinner at *The Lodge*, the only fine dining establishment in Comfort Valley.

They spared no expense, course after course of savory plates rotating on and off the table as the wait staff delivered each item with a detailed description and a little bow. Noah didn't frequent fancy places like this often, so it was a real treat, no matter how out of his element he felt. He wondered if wining and dining was routine for Oliver and Samantha. He figured their jobs required evenings much like this one.

As they finished their meals, Noah noticed a younger couple rise from the secluded booth behind the family's long table. He had assumed they were out-of-towners, maybe even newlyweds, from the way the woman kept glancing toward the glittering diamond perched on her finger like it was a new accessory she hadn't quite gotten used to.

After the man had paid their check, he led his date to a small area where a bedecked Christmas tree glinted with lights and crystal ornaments. It was intimate and cozy and suddenly gave Noah an idea.

"What do you think?" he turned to Marty and nudged his chin toward the vacant piano at the back corner of the establishment. "You up for a little post-dinner serenading?"

"I'll see what I can come up with." Marty threaded his fingers together and pushed out, popping his knuckles one by one. Then he quickly stood and left for the piano bench.

As soon as his fingertips traced over the keys, the

couple lit up in appreciation. Those first notes of *Rocking Around the Christmas Tree* emitting from the grand instrument effortlessly summoned the rest of the restaurant patrons. It wasn't long before all were on their feet, shimmying and shaking their way to the makeshift dance floor to join in on the fun.

Just as Noah was about to approach Samantha, Oliver intercepted him.

"Care to dance?" Oliver asked, eclipsing Noah completely.

Samantha's gaze skirted around her ex, a remorseful expression meeting Noah's. "Next one," she mouthed as she passed by. She caught and squeezed his hand reassuringly.

Noah smiled, realizing he would have to pivot both in direction and intent, otherwise he'd be left alone while everyone else whirled and twirled around him.

"Grandma." He held out an upturned hand. "Would you like to share this dance?"

"Oh, Noah. You know I'd love to." Kitty slapped her palm down into his and tugged him across the room. "But are you sure you can keep up?"

"I'll do my best."

The fast tempo was no issue for Grandma Kitty, an absolute force on the dance floor. She moved her arms and legs, kicking out her feet in time with the lively rhythm. By the end of the song, even Noah was winded, but Kitty kept at it all through *Holly Jolly Christmas* and *Jingle Bells*, her bursting energy never waning. When Marty finally downshifted to *The First Noel*, Kitty took a breath and looked up at her grandson.

"That's what you've been waiting for. Something a little slower," she acknowledged as she patted his chest. "I'll sit this one out. You go find your girl."

Like his earlier conversation with Thomas, Noah wanted to tell his grandma that Samantha wasn't his, and his lips parted just enough to form the first words. But when he scanned the room to track Samantha down, Noah didn't need words to make that truth known. Oliver was already at work proving it.

They were pressed close together within the throng of swaying couples. Samantha's head nestled affectionately between Oliver's neck and shoulder, eyes slipped shut like she was blissfully at home in his embrace. Oliver's hands trailed up and down her back in a way that made Noah's throat clog with emotion. He coughed, hoping to clear the burn, but the bitter taste of envy tinged his mouth.

Noah skirted the dance floor, his eyes and focus locked in on one thing only: the restaurant's exit.

"Hey brother—" David looked up from Vera in his arms, but Noah waved him off.

Keys already in hand, Noah strode across the parking lot in a jog that was close to an all-out run.

This was why he didn't do relationships. Why he didn't date and why he rarely pursued anything romantic with the few women he did go out with.

Things were too complicated at his age. Baggage was inevitable. Exes were a given.

But an ex-husband who was still clearly in love with his once wife? That was more baggage than an airport luggage conveyer. Noah just couldn't compete.

He fit his keys into the ignition once inside the vehicle and the engine rumbled to life. Ice blurred the windshield. Even with the defroster cranked to full blast, his vision was completely obstructed. All he wanted was to rush home and erase the sight of Samantha and Oliver from his memory. Scrub it from his brain.

"Oh, come on. Would you hurry up?" he hissed at the Jeep.

He flipped the windshield wipers on, but they did little to clear the opaque haze.

"Noah!" David's fist met the window. "Noah, open up."

"Not right now, David." Noah shook his head, chest humming with irritation. He knew his frustration was misplaced, but his head wasn't on straight. He needed some time alone.

"Noah, open up!"

"David, leave me—"

It was then that the wipers swept the last of the ice aside and Vera suddenly came into view. She clutched her stomach with one hand, the hood of the Jeep with the other, and her face contorted with a grimace that made even Noah wince.

He stretched across the cab and threw open his passenger side door.

"What's going on?"

"Contractions." David ushered his wife into the vehicle and then climbed into the back seat. "Marty drove us all here in the van, but I don't think it'll make it to the hospital as fast as your Jeep can. Plus, she keeps insisting we let him play."

"Everyone is having such a nice time. I don't want to be the one to ruin that," Vera said before another contraction took over. She wailed loudly enough to stir Big Cody out of hibernation.

"I called the hospital," David said. He reached over the front seat and squeezed his wife's shoulders, but she shrugged him off as she doubled over with the force of another contracting wave. "They're ready for us. I just need you to get us there. And fast."

TEXT BUBBLES PULSED ACROSS NOAH'S SCREEN. He'd kept his phone on silent while in the waiting room at the hospital, but now that he was back at home, he flipped the sound switch on again. At that instant, a loud trill echoed from the device.

Samantha: *How's she doing?*

Physically? Noah replied. *Seems to be fine. But David said she's pretty disappointed they sent her home. She was more than ready to meet her new little one.*

The bubbles repeated.

Samantha: *I've heard false labor is pretty common. Especially with your first. Is there anything they need?*

Noah: *I think a good night's sleep is what the doctor ordered.*

Samantha: *Well, will you let them know I'm here if there's any way I can help?*

Will do, Noah typed back.

He tossed his phone onto his nightstand with a clatter and folded his arms underneath his head, eyes glued to the ceiling. He didn't like this—their superficial conversation. Did Samantha sense it, too? The mounting tension between them? It wasn't as though she was aware Noah glimpsed her dancing with Oliver, but it also wasn't like she had tried to hide her contentedness while in her ex-husband's arms.

Noah supposed he was glad he had a plausible cover for his behavior. When Samantha had texted asking why he'd left in such a rush, Noah explained about Vera's contractions. He didn't have to come clean with the fact that he'd not only acted impulsively, but immaturely, too, when he saw the exes slow dancing. Truth was, it was more sadness than anger that had enveloped him, squeezing him so tightly he'd feared tears would spill right out.

His phone pinged again.

Samantha: *How are you doing? Is there anything you need?*

'To stop acting like a jealous teenager,' Noah half-considered texting back. Instead, he just punched out, *I'm fine.*

Samantha: *I know it's late, but would I be able to come up for a few minutes? There's something I'd like to show you.*

He needed a good night's sleep to distance himself from the evening and his thoughts, but he also knew his time with Samantha was limited. Before long, she'd be heading back to Sacramento and he would be wishing for more moments with her.

Of course, he replied, and within five minutes, there was a knock on his door.

"Hi." Her smile was as bright as the crescent mood that hung directly above her. "Can I come in?"

"Absolutely." Noah stepped to the side to allow her to pass. "Thank you again for dinner tonight. You guys really went all out and while it wasn't necessary, it was appreciated."

"It's the least we could do." She shrugged. "Well, I guess making a snowman was the least we could do. I'm really sorry we ruined the festivities."

"You didn't ruin anything." Noah moved to the couch and for a moment, he feared Samantha would take the old leather chair opposite him. When she lowered to the cushion beside him, he breathed a relieved sigh. Maybe the tension was all on his end, fabricated and untrue. "Is there a reason you guys didn't play along?"

"I was prepared to. I'm sure you saw my armful of supplies. I fully intended to annihilate the competition with the best snowman the Jensen family has ever seen," she said with a single laugh. "But Oliver decided our time would be better spent rehashing past hurts and picking at old wounds."

"Oh, Samantha." Noah touched her arm.

"It's okay. Really, it is. We worked things out."

Noah swallowed down his growing insecurities. He had to be a bigger man than the one he'd been earlier in the evening when he'd stormed out of the restaurant in a flurry of confused emotion. He didn't wear jealousy well.

"I'm glad you two have been able to work things out," he willed himself to say. "You said all along you wanted Oliver to do something with the second chance life has given him. A second chance at a life—with you—sure seems like the best use of it."

Samantha's upper half twisted, suddenly squared off with Noah on the sofa. "What?"

"I saw you two dancing. It's obvious there's still something there."

With a huff, Samantha shook her head. "I meant we worked things out professionally." Eyes narrowed, she pinned Noah with a stare he felt shoot all the way through his stomach. "We're dividing up the agency."

"You're what?"

"Oliver still has feelings for me, Noah. At least he thinks he does. I'm worried our close proximity in the workplace has somehow made him unable to move on. He's suddenly ready for a family and for some reason, he thinks I'm the one he wants that with." She gathered Noah's hands into her grip. "I don't want that."

"You don't?"

"No, I don't," she said. "Don't get me wrong. I want those things. A family and a future with someone, but that someone isn't Oliver."

They sat there a moment, eyes locked, hearts racing. Well, Noah's was, at least. He couldn't be sure Samantha's was thrumming the same staccato beat, but he sensed it by the way they mirrored one another completely in the moment. There was an unspoken hope passing between them, and even though all she did was reach out and lay her hand upon his, it affirmed everything.

"I have something for you."

Slipping her hand back, Samantha pulled out a small flash drive from her coat pocket and dropped it into Noah's palm. "I hope it means as much to you as it does to me."

CHAPTER 27

*S*amantha had watched the commercial no less than a dozen times, and with every viewing, she noticed something new. Something that made her bubble with joy. Something that made goosebumps rise on her flesh, tickled by the sheer magic of it all.

The way the aerial shots swept out and over the ridge, zooming above snow-capped treetops before coasting leisurely upon the cabins, felt exactly like taking a ride on Santa's sleigh.

Filming the commercial from Santa Claus's perspective had ultimately been her father's idea. The lens became Santa's eye as the footage rolled throughout the property, highlighting all areas—and people—of importance. The check-in lodge where Vera dangled a set of brass keys into an outstretched, white-gloved hand. The kitchen where the camera caught Santa reaching for a spatula drenched in peppermint fudge, only to be swatted away by Grandma Kitty, who waggled a crooked finger at the lens. He joined Audrey at the piano, the camera focused on their four hands roving over the keyboard, matching the notes of Marty's holiday composition that played on a track throughout the entire commercial.

And, of course, there was Noah. He hadn't been an intentional actor in the spot like the others had, but he made his debut all the same. The camera was stationed just outside the woodshop window, peering in as though Santa himself was stealing a glimpse of Noah hard at work fashioning Christmas toys.

This was the part Samantha had been most concerned with, particularly because she hadn't gotten Noah's approval to film him while he worked privately. It was an 'ask forgiveness rather than permission' sort of thing, and she hoped she'd made the right decision.

But the ending—that was her favorite part. The camera angles retreated back and the drone took over once more, mimicking Santa returning to flight on his sleigh. Then the words, *"Not all of Santa's helpers work at the North Pole"* rolled across the screen as Trish's soothing voice read the phrase aloud and invited viewers to learn more about booking a magical holiday stay at Cedar Crest Cabins by visiting the listed website.

The marketing piece was everything it needed to

be: informative, entertaining, and chock-full of Christmas splendor.

If a commercial was the last remaining hope for the cabins, this was the precise one to deliver that. But the fact that it was nearing noon and she'd yet to hear from Noah made something in Samantha's chest catch.

Had they gotten it all wrong? Admittedly, it was a one-eighty from the original script she'd been presented with. But going a completely different direction was the only real option. The commercial needed to focus on the Jensen family. They were the true heart of it all.

On multiple occasions, Samantha had reached for her phone to compose a text, but she ultimately thought it best to wait on Noah instead. If he hated it, he likely needed time to construct a respectful way to deliver that disappointing news.

But if he loved it? Well, that would mean the world to Samantha.

She sighed as she stood at the cabin window, committing the wintery scene to memory. In two days, that's all it would be.

"I'm just not ready," she spoke under a breath.

Not ready to leave Cedar Crest. Not ready to figure out the division of Knight and Day. Not ready for this next, uncertain chapter set out before her.

But readiness wasn't a requirement in life. She hadn't been ready to find love, and that's exactly what had happened here at Cedar Crest. With the cabins.

With Noah. She loved him. And whether or not that love was reciprocated, she would allow her heart to feel it because it was real and true and undeniable.

She tugged her plaid shawl around her shoulders like a hug and looked about the room, every piece of it already feeling more like home than her empty house in the suburbs. She supposed a little of that had to do with the fact that everything within the cabin reminded her of Noah. The tree with the lights they'd untangled and strung, along with the popcorn garland that wove in and out of the lush branches. The coffee table where her half-consumed bottle of wine rested. The wine she knew he'd hated but still tried, if only because she'd mentioned it was her favorite. The couch where they'd shared their hearts and a kiss…

There was a knock at the door.

She raced to it, praying with urgency that the man she'd been thinking of so fondly stood on the other side.

"Noah!" she praised. She flung her arms around his neck.

"That's one heck of a greeting."

"I just really, really wanted it to be you." She pulled him into the room, almost abandoning her earlier worry about his reaction to the commercial.

"Then I'm glad I could deliver." He looked at her inquisitively, eyebrow arched to a point. "Is everything okay?"

"Yes. Everything is great." It was now that he was here, with her. She summoned every ounce of her confidence when she asked, "Did you have a chance to watch the commercial yet?"

"I did."

"And?"

"And…" The single word lingered between them.

"You hate it."

"I don't hate it."

Samantha flopped backward onto the couch in the exasperation of defeat. "I can take it. Tell me. All of it. The brutal truth. Don't hold back."

"It's hard to find the words—"

"For something so awful." Her hand smothered her eyes.

Even though she shielded herself, she could sense Noah sit next to her, his presence palpable at her side.

"It's hard to find the words,"—He withdrew her hand from her face and kept it in his—"for perfection."

"It's not quite perfect," Samantha disclosed.

"Maybe not entirely, but it perfectly conveys the essence of this place. The people. What makes Cedar Crest special. It's more than *anything* I could have hoped for." He tugged her hand closer, pulling her from the sunken cushion so their chests pressed together. "And you're *everything* I could have hoped for."

Then his lips met hers in the sweetest chaste kiss that left her breathless despite the brevity of it.

"I have something for you." He stood quickly. "It's just outside the door. Mind if I go get it?"

"Not at all."

While Noah retrieved the item, Samantha moved toward the small storage closet near the cabin's bathroom. She'd stowed Noah's Christmas gift there after Marty had delivered it to her earlier that morning. She was indebted to Noah's older brother for so many reasons: for the time he spent composing the commercial music and now for the hours he'd used up in the woodshop, crafting the perfect box for her holiday surprise.

For some gifts, plain cardboard packaging was a suitable option, but not for this one. This particular gift—she hoped—would be a lasting keepsake for Noah. Something he would pull out and use year after year. A proper wooden box was the only fitting wrapping.

She spun around when the front door clicked open and she shoved the box behind her back.

"I really hope you like it," Noah noted as he crossed the room. His eyes were on the lovely poinsettia printed gift bag in his hands. "I'm not as talented with a chisel and a block of wood as my dad and grandpa were, but I gave it a valiant effort."

Arm outstretched, he held the bag by its red grosgrain strings for Samantha to take.

"I have something for you, too," she acknowledged. She swung the large box out and around to her middle.

"Samantha, you didn't have to—"

"Of course, I didn't have to. That's what makes it

a gift, silly." She grinned with mischievous delight. "Plus, I'm beginning to think gift giving might be my love language. Just like Kitty's. I've been so excited to give this to you, I can hardly stand it. I know it's not Christmas just yet, but I want you to have this before the big day."

"I'd have to agree with you on that—about the whole love language thing," he said. "All the time you spent on our commercial is a bigger gift than any of us Jensens could ever possibly deserve."

"I would argue that you all deserve so much more. But instead of arguing, let's get to opening." She traded off the large box for the gift bag. "You go first."

"You sure?"

"Yes. I'm going to combust if I have to keep this to myself much longer."

"Well, we wouldn't want that."

Noah lowered the box to the nearby coffee table and gingerly withdrew the wooden lid, his move-ments slow and purposeful, as though he somehow already understood the importance of the present and wanted to relish in it. Samantha didn't look down at the item, but kept her eyes trained on Noah's face. She was eager to catch his expression the very moment he read the card perched on top of the gift.

"*May you never be too old to search the skies on Christmas Eve…*"

He lifted the piece of parchment and glimpsed the

gift nestled beneath it on a bed of crinkled, kraft paper shavings. "Is it—?"

"A drone," she cut off, eager to explain the real meaning behind it all. "The very one used to film most of the commercial."

"Samantha, that is so thoughtful. Thank you." He brushed an affectionate kiss against the apple of her cheek.

"You're welcome, but it's actually more than just a drone," she detailed. She picked up the electronic device to turn it over. "I'm not sure if you're aware, but most drones have a flashing light. Sometimes they are green, sometimes white, but with this particular drone, it's red."

Noah lifted his eyes to Samantha's.

"It's your sleigh, Noah. Complete with Rudolph and his glowing, red nose."

A mist came over Noah's gaze and she noted his throat pulse with an emotional swallow. "Samantha, I…I have no words…"

"I know what a special tradition it was for you, Noah. And even though you can't fly your dad's plane on Christmas Eve, it's nice that new ways exist to carry out old memories."

So swiftly she didn't see it coming, Noah threw his arms around her in a hug that squeezed the very breath from her lungs. "I love it," he murmured into her hair, his words cracking with heartfelt passion. "And I love you."

"I love you, too."

It was a relief to utter the words aloud. The words that had tinkered around in her heart all week until they'd settled into her being like a long-held truth.

"Your turn." He pushed the box aside and nudged toward her gift bag.

Samantha dipped her hand into the tissue paper, digging around until her grasp landed on the carving. She pulled it out.

"They're supposed to be snowshoes," he said.

She could see it, the way the wooden figurine was whittled to resemble a pair of snowshoes, one shoe crossed over the other.

"It almost looks like a heart," she noticed, her lips tugging upward. "The way they overlap like so. You did a beautiful job."

"I'm glad that translates, because that's exactly what it's supposed to look like," Noah said. "And like your gift to me, there's an explanation that goes along with it. The other day, I was over at my friend's house, an older gentleman named Thomas Ridley."

"We met him at the hardware store."

"We did. His wife, Bessie, well, her health is failing, and she doesn't have much time left."

"Oh, I'm very sorry to hear that."

Noah acknowledged her condolence with a gentle smile. "Thomas likened their life to a downhill ski run. Said they were on their last part of their run together. That stuck with me. But you know what? I think life is a lot more like cross-country snowshoeing than it is downhill skiing. At least, I want mine to be that way. I don't want it to pass me by, only catching the beauty and the scenery out of my periphery as it flashes around me. I want to take my time and appreciate where I am and who I'm with throughout all of it," he said. "And I want you to be the person to accompany me on that journey, Samantha. I don't know what that will look like, what with me living up here and you in Sacramento, but I'm willing to do whatever it takes to make that work. To make us work."

She pressed two flat palms to Noah's chest and rose onto her toes, her lips tenderly meeting his.

"I know exactly what it will look like," she said. "It will be compromise and planning and hoping and dreaming, but we'll do all of that together. I'm up for the hard work of making our dreams—and our future —a reality, Noah."

She stepped out of his embrace, hands landing on her hips before adding, "Just as long as we're not *actually* snowshoeing. Because you say you don't want life to pass you by, but I'm fairly certain you don't want it to slog along at the dreadfully slow snowshoeing pace you know I'm capable of."

"That's where you're wrong. I'd freeze every moment of my life with you if I could." He kissed her once more, slowly and thoughtfully.

"I'm all for that." Samantha angled to meet Noah's lips again, fully in agreement that each moment should be savored, cherished, and enjoyed. Starting with this very one.

"*H*ow's my little one doing?"

Vera peered over Samantha's shoulder to glimpse the sweet baby in her lap, so bundled up in warm layers that she very nearly resembled a marshmallow puff. Samantha bounced her niece on her knee just as the little girl began to fuss.

"She's doing great," Samantha said. "Loves the fire. Keeps staring at it as it pops and crackles. I think it's keeping her entertained."

"Well, I appreciate *you* keeping her entertained while I see to it that the actual entertainment is taken care of. I think they're finally ready to take the stage."

It was the perfect evening for a small, open-air concert, their last of the season at Cedar Crest, in fact. The December night, while crisp, was balmy enough that one wouldn't shiver while sitting under the starry skies, enjoying an evening of acoustic music in the mountains.

It had been one of Samantha's greatest delights to line up the weekly talent, finishing the concert series off with Marty and Trish as the season's closing act.

She hadn't been on the hunt for talent in well over a year, and while she sometimes missed her role at the agency, she now found greater purpose outside of the workplace.

Some ten months earlier, Oliver had propositioned Samantha with an offer to buy her out completely rather than divide up Knight and Day. It didn't take much mulling over to know it was a lucrative deal she couldn't refuse, especially since it resulted in funds she could funnel directly into the cabins, their restoration, and hopefully, future expansion.

Noah hadn't loved the idea at first. He wasn't entirely comfortable accepting Samantha's monetary contribution, particularly in such a large lump sum. But once Samantha had gently reminded him that—as a married couple—what was hers was his and what was his was hers, he softened a little. They shared everything else already. Their money should also fall right in step.

Of course, Noah's hesitation wasn't completely unwarranted. Before her marriage to Oliver, Samantha hadn't signed a prenuptial agreement, and it was something she often thought would have been beneficial, given the unfortunate way things ended. Noah was aware of this, and his reluctance to merge their accounts and finances likely stemmed from that knowledge. He wanted to protect her in that way, but

Samantha was a firm believer that you didn't go into things planning for their failure. Nope. Like she always said, "Prepare for success by planning to celebrate it."

And that's exactly what their wedding and resulting marriage had been: a celebration of love, family, and faith. Samantha felt like popping a bottle of champagne each and every day, but with her recently expanding belly, she opted for sparkling cider instead.

"Can I get you anything before I check in on Marty and Trish one last time? Tea? Ginger ale?" Vera asked. "I remember how nauseous I was my first trimester."

"I'm good for now. But thank you."

Little Caroline babbled an incoherent trill of joy. Samantha squeezed her close. She couldn't wait to hold her own child in her arms, but spending time with her niece helped to satisfy that ache.

There were so many times she'd worried she had missed her opportunity to have her own child, especially once the divorce had been finalized. She couldn't envision a future where she would be gifted with the chance to become a mother.

She had so much to be grateful for that at Thanksgiving dinner the month before, she could have gone on for hours when it came her time to share her blessings. Life was full, love was abundant, and family was everything.

Overcome, Samantha felt her chin tremble as

unshed tears pricked her eyes. Caroline's chubby hand reached up and cupped Samantha's cheek, and that was enough to release just a single tear. It sloped over the curves of her face and Samantha had to sniff back her emotion.

"Hey." Noah hunkered down onto the empty Adirondack chair next to them, grunting a little with the effort. He caught sight of Samantha's wet cheek and his eyes widened. "Sweetheart, are you okay?"

"These are happy tears."

"We have a lot to be happy about. I'll give you that." He rubbed his hands together and placed his palms out to warm them against the flickering orange flames in the fire pit several feet away. "Did I tell you yet that one more nomination came in today? It's for a family from the Bay Area. Their dad is coming back from a year of serving overseas and he's going to meet them here on Christmas Eve as a surprise. Their neighbors nominated them and want to cover all the costs. Room and board. All of it. With the addition of this family, we'll be at capacity come Christmas and everything has been covered by grants and donations."

"Oh, that's wonderful, Noah." If she wasn't careful, all of this good news was going to turn her into a blubbering ball of emotion she couldn't quell. "And once construction starts this spring on the four additional cabins, we'll have even more space to bless even more people."

"Exactly what Dad and Grandpa would have wanted," Noah said. "I'm sure of it."

"So am I."

Just then, Marty's fingers hit the keyboard, pulling the attention of the crowd gathered around the hillside fire pits and drawing their gazes up toward the front of the amphitheater.

"Merry Christmas, Cedar Crest!" Trish Whitley stepped onto the stage, gloved hand waving in the air, red lipstick lined smile spread from ear to ear. "Are you all ready to get a little jolly around here?"

A group of children rushed to the front to form a cluster at the base of the stage, their hands outstretched as Trish reached down to shake each one. She was a natural, belting it out as she engaged with her audience that knew every word to her recent holiday single.

Trish and Marty's Christmas album rested solidly in the top ten on the charts. There were multiple reasons for their success. Marty was a sensation at the piano. Samantha had always believed that, and it was nice to see others finally recognize it, too. And, of course, Trish had the voice of an angel, one lending itself perfectly to this sort of Christmas music.

But it was their chemistry that likely garnered more than a few fans. Everyone loved a good celebrity romance, and Marty and Trish's was proving to be just that. Something came alive in Marty when he played for Trish, and Trish never sounded better than when accompanied by Marty's expertise on the piano.

It was the most beautiful pairing of talent Samantha had matched yet. The perfect one to retire on.

Leaning forward, she bounced Caroline on her lap in time with the cheerful chorus. The baby's rhythm was all off, wobbling and bobbing, but feeling the music all the same. Samantha smiled at the sweet innocence of it all.

Once Trish finished her first song, an original, Marty started in on the familiar notes of *Santa Claus is Coming to Town*, and the gaggle of kids at the ledge of the platform erupted with shrieks and cheers, knowing exactly what would come next.

From the back corner of the stage, Jack Day emerged, donned in red and white from head to toe, gripping a large velvet sack thrown over his right shoulder. He was perfect, the sort of Santa that gave you no reason not to believe.

Certainly, all the kids believed. They jumped up and down, flapping their arms to wave him near. Even Caroline leapt with delight. Jack crouched down to their level, slinging the bag around to loosen the gold drawstring.

Trish crooned behind him, encouraging the crowd to sing along as Jack started to hand out toys to each child. Carved wooden toys.

The Jensen men had been hard at work throughout summer and most of autumn. They didn't want to run out, Noah had said. There had been a high demand for their wooden figures, especially after the cabin's commercial aired last year. The shot of Noah carving in the woodshed struck a chord with many viewers, particularly the ones who had visited Cedar Crest decades earlier as children. They received letters and emails, many saying they still had their Cedar Crest toys. Some asked if they could purchase a custom one for their own child. Others reached out, wishing to stock their shops and stores with these Jensen originals.

It was everything to see Noah take the lead on this. They made trains and nutcrackers, bears and dolls. Every sort of nostalgic children's toy one could imagine, they carved it. The woodshop overflowed, and so did Samantha's heart when she glimpsed her husband's joy.

This was legacy lived out, and it was the most beautiful sight.

As the merry song neared its last notes, Jack handed off the last of the toys. Turning to go, he passed off one final gift to Marty, leaving it to rest on the top of the piano. Marty winked, then raced his fingers up and down the keys to match the grand ending notes as Trish belted them out. This was the point in the set where she would walk toward the front to engage with her audience while Marty typically gave his fingers a rest before the next song. But he didn't do that.

Instead, he took the small wooden box from the piano's ledge and came up behind Trish, dropping to one knee, visible to all in the audience but out of sight to Trish. A collective gasp resounded, yet Trish was utterly unaware.

"You all having a good time out there?" she hollered. "Ready for one more?"

Noah swung his gaze toward Samantha, eyes wide with the dawning of understanding. "Is he doing what I think he is?"

Samantha nodded. "I think he sure is."

"Oh my goodness. Oh my goodness!" Vera came up behind Samantha, scooping her daughter from her sister-in-law's lap. David was right at her side, and Audrey and Grandma Kitty stood behind them both. "Is this really happening?"

"I do believe it is." Noah rose to his feet, along with most everyone in the crowd. He moved toward Samantha and curled his arm around her waist to hug her close.

Anticipation buzzed around them, something Trish likely mistook for typical concert energy. She kept up the conversation with her fans, chattering away about their next song and how it held a special place in her heart.

"If you know the words, feel free to sing along."

She spun around, all but toppling over Marty, who was down on bended knee.

The microphone fell from her grasp, clattering to the ground with a shrill, hollow pierce.

"Marty!" The discarded microphone picked up her voice, even from a few feet away. "Yes!" She dropped to his level and cupped his jaw with her hands, smothering his lips with a kiss. Samantha wasn't even sure he had gotten out the words yet, but Trish didn't wait for the formal proposal to give her answer. "Yes! Of course, yes!" she exclaimed again.

"Well, would you look at that?" Noah murmured close to Samantha's ear. "Marty finally finds love. It's like our very own Christmas miracle."

Samantha snuggled into her husband's side. "I'm beginning to believe miracles are more common than we realize." She rested her head upon his shoulder and breathed in his rich and familiar scent of bergamot and pine. "If you look for them, you'll find them."

"I wholeheartedly agree with you on that," Noah said. "And whether it was a miracle, fate, or an answer to a Christmas wish that landed you here at the cabins and ultimately in my arms, I'll take it. It's the best gift I've ever been given."

"I think maybe it was a little of all of those things," she said. Her gaze moved across the mountainside, from the surrounding crowd to the stage before them, to the trees and cresting hills that hemmed everything in. "It's a magical life we have here, isn't it?"

"It certainly is," Noah said. "And I can't wait to create even more magic as we spend the rest of our lives together, side by side, hand in hand. Merry Christmas, Samantha. I love you with everything I am."

Samantha threaded her fingers with his, her heart

full of love for this incredible place, these caring people, and for the future she knew would be the one of her dreams.

"I love you too, Noah. Merry Christmas."

THE END

Also by Megan Squires
Christmas at Yuletide Farm
An Heirloom Christmas
A Lake House Holiday
In the Market for Love

Join Megan Squires' Reader Group!
Join my corner of Facebook where I share sneak peeks, host giveaways, and get to know my readers even better!

To stay up to date on new releases, please sign up for Megan's newsletter:

http://subscribe.megansquiresauthor.com

ABOUT THE AUTHOR

Growing up with only a lizard for a pet, Megan Squires now makes up for it by caring for the nearly forty animals on her twelve-acre flower farm in Northern California. A UC Davis graduate, Megan worked in the political non-profit realm prior to becoming a stay-at-home mom. She then spent nearly ten years as an award winning photographer, with her work published in magazines such as Professional Photographer and Click.

In 2012, her creativity took a turn when she wrote and published her first young adult novel. Megan is both traditionally and self-published and *A Winter Cabin Christmas* is her fourteenth publication. She can't go a day without Jesus, her family and farm animals, and a large McDonald's Diet Coke.

To keep up with Megan online, please visit:

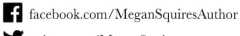 facebook.com/MeganSquiresAuthor

 twitter.com/MeganSquires

instagram.com/megansquiresauthor